Scottish
Bakehouse
Mysteries™

Tartan Feathered

Jan Fields

Annie's®
AnniesFiction.com

Books in the Scottish Bakehouse Mysteries series

. . . and more to come!

Library of Congress-in-Publication Data
Tartan Feathered / by Jan Fields
p. cm.
I. Title
                    2020938139

AnniesFiction.com
(800) 282-6643
Scottish Bakehouse Mysteries™
Series Creator: Shari Lohner
Series Editor: Elizabeth Morrissey
Cover Illustrator: Kelley McMorris

10 11 12 13 14 | Printed in China | 9 8 7 6 5 4 3 2

1

Without taking her eyes from the book in her hand, Molly Ferris tugged the knitted afghan from the back of the couch and pulled it over her lap. She wasn't sure if she needed to raise the temperature in her apartment or if the shivers were from the mystery. When Grizela Duff had practically forced the book on Molly, the Scotland-born librarian had insisted it was a *braw* tale. Now that she was reading it, Molly wasn't sure about brilliant, but it was certainly scary.

Though she had no proof, she suspected Grizela had chosen this particular novel as a lesson. Like several other residents of Loch Mallaig, Michigan, Grizela thought Molly's curiosity sent her and her best friends—Laura Donovan and Carol MacCallan—into danger a bit too often, much like the amateur sleuth in the story whose clue following had steered her into a terrifying climax.

Molly jumped as something fuzzy touched her foot. She peered over her book to see her beloved Scottish terrier, Angus, with one paw on her leg and his beloved toy, Woolie, held carefully in his jaws.

"You want up here?" she asked.

The little Scottie shifted excitedly, his black eyes shining. Angus could make the jump onto the sofa normally, but the stuffed sheep was clearly enough of an encumbrance to make him hesitant.

Molly leaned over to scoop him up and deposit him beside her. "Luckily for you, I can use the company while I read this."

Angus snuggled into the afghan with Woolie and closed his eyes.

"Be glad you don't read," Molly told her pup. "I doubt I'll be able to close my eyes tonight."

If Angus felt sorry for her, he showed no sign. Molly returned to the book. The current scene had the main character being chased across the Highland moors by a shadowy villain. Within moments, the world had fallen away around her, and she was practically holding her breath as the threatening figure closed the gap. Bony fingers caught in the young woman's auburn curls. At the exact instant the heroine screamed, Angus burst into a frenzy of barking, making Molly shriek in surprise.

Angus leaped from the sofa and rushed out of the apartment's sitting room. Molly tossed the book onto the afghan and followed him, her heart pounding. She found Angus barking at the door that led to the building's interior stairs. "What is it, Angus?"

If the little dog had an answer, he didn't offer it. He merely put his front feet up on the door and pawed insistently, as if he could scratch the door open.

"If you've nearly given me a heart attack over a mouse," Molly warned, "you won't get a scrap of Thanksgiving leftovers."

But when she opened the door, Molly heard banging on the back entrance of Bread on Arrival, the Scottish bakehouse she lived above and co-owned with Laura and Carol. The grand Victorian house was formerly a funeral parlor—hence the bakery's name—and featured the kitchen and café downstairs with Molly's living quarters and the bakery office upstairs.

Wondering who could be pounding on the door this late in the evening, Molly hurried down the steps with Angus close enough to make him a tripping hazard. When they reached the downstairs hall, Angus rocketed toward the door. Even over his wild barking, Molly could recognize the voice calling from outside. "Mom!"

Molly fumbled with the lock in her excitement, then flung open the door. "Chloe!" She threw her arms around her daughter and hugged her tightly over the threshold. "What a wonderful surprise! I thought you couldn't come until after Thanksgiving."

With Chloe working as a veterinarian in Milwaukee and Molly living in Michigan's Upper Peninsula, they didn't get to spend nearly as much time together as either would have preferred.

Chloe laughed at her mom's excitement and Angus's dancing around them. "I didn't think I could either, but the clinic had to close down."

"What happened?" Molly reluctantly released Chloe from the hug, but kept her gaze on her. The beautiful young woman's appearance was a fifty-fifty blend of her parents, but in this light, she looked so much like her father that tears nearly sprang to Molly's eyes. Her late husband, Kevin, had suffered a fatal reaction to antibiotics more than ten years earlier, but occasionally she still felt the sting of his passing.

"There are bats in the belfry," Chloe said as she lifted her suitcase from the stoop. "Or rather, the attic crawl space. I didn't want to wake the whole neighborhood, but you weren't answering your phone."

"I'm sorry. It was in the other room." Once Chloe was inside, Molly shut the door and flipped the lock into place. "Come on up and tell me all about the clinic."

"We heard scrabbling noises overhead and called animal control," Chloe explained as she followed her mother upstairs. "That's when we discovered bats had decided to winter over in the clinic's attic. We aren't sure how they got in, but a couple of the bats tested positive for rabies. We had to clear out all our patients until it is dealt with and we can be sure no bats will reenter. I'm free for at least a week, probably a couple days more with the holiday."

"I'll hope for the extra days since it's exactly a week until Thanksgiving." Molly waved Chloe into the kitchenette. "Can I make you dinner?"

"No thanks. I stopped on the way."

"As cold as it is outside, you should at least have a hot drink. I could fix hot chocolate."

Chloe smiled. "With marshmallows?"

"Homemade marshmallows even," Molly said with a grin. "I bought some at a fall bake sale last week. I'd never had them before, but they're delicious."

"Sounds perfect." Chloe peered around the tiny kitchenette. "This is cozy. Maybe too cozy. I should get a room somewhere nearby. Do you have any recommendations?"

"Of course, if you need your own space," Molly said. "But you're welcome to stay here. You can have my room, and I'll sleep on the pullout."

"I am not taking your bed," Chloe insisted. "But the pullout is perfectly fine."

Molly showed Chloe around the apartment, regaling her with tales of the cow-themed wallpaper and mauve paint that had decorated it when she, Carol, and Laura had bought the place. Now it featured a serene blue-and-white color scheme with Molly's tasteful, comfortable furnishings, and there wasn't a cow in sight.

Molly left Chloe in the cozy den to settle in, then returned to the kitchen and poured milk into a pot to start their hot cocoa. As she was stirring the milk in the pan, Chloe walked in holding the book Molly had been reading. "Is this any good?"

"If you don't mind nightmares," Molly said.

Chloe blinked in surprise. "I didn't think you cared for scary books or movies."

"The head librarian here forced it on me. And when I return books, sometimes there's a pop quiz. No one wants to get a scolding from Grizela Duff."

Chloe chuckled. "Trust my mom to be afraid of a librarian."

Molly pointed at her with the spoon. "You scoff, but if you met Grizela, you'd understand." She watched Chloe read the cover of the novel and wondered if the lighting in her kitchenette was making Chloe's face shadowed. "Have you been getting enough sleep?"

Chloe glanced up and raised her eyebrows. "I'm not the one who wakes before dawn every day because she opened a bakery with her college best friends thirty years after graduation. Or who makes a habit of skulking around in the dark searching for clues."

Molly frowned. "It's not a habit and don't avoid the question."

Chloe shrugged. "The practice has been busy, and we've added more night hours to accommodate clients who work. As the junior member of the staff, I pick up a lot of those hours. When you add a limited social life to that, I'm not surprised I look a little tired. Especially to my eagle-eyed mother."

"You can sleep in every day here if you want. The only thing that will wake you up is the smell of Laura's cinnamon rolls wafting up through the ventilation system."

"That sounds wonderful. Both the sleep and the cinnamon rolls." Chloe glanced toward the pot. "The milk is about to boil."

"Yikes." Molly spun around sharply and quickly added the ingredients for hot cocoa.

While she worked, Chloe sauntered over to the small table and chairs and sank into one, setting the book on the table. "Honestly, I'm grateful for the time off," Chloe said. "And, of course, I'm glad to see you."

Molly grinned at her as she dropped marshmallows into each

mug. "Good save." She carried the mugs to the table and took the seat across from Chloe. For a moment, they both sat quietly, enjoying the hot, rich beverage and gazing out the window.

"I won't press you on it," Molly said finally, "but I hope you'll eventually tell me what's bothering you."

Chloe set the cup down. "Are you that good or am I that transparent?"

"You never were one to hide your feelings. Besides, it's a mom's job to know when something's up with her daughter," Molly said before taking another sip of cocoa. She let silence fall between them and resisted the urge to push. When Chloe didn't speak, Molly broke and added, "If you're having trouble at work, I think Loch Mallaig could use another vet." *So much for not pressing her.*

Chloe gazed at her mother over the rim of her mug. "It's not the practice, though that definitely keeps me on my toes. I'm glad for the break, but I love the clinic. My coworkers are great, and I love every single one of our patients." She rolled her eyes. "Now their owners can be a handful sometimes, but I like them anyway."

"If it's not your work life . . ." Molly let her words hang in the air.

"Fine, it's my love life. I went out a few times with a guy named Camden Landry," Chloe said, her expression glum. "We met when I treated his dog, a sweet schnauzer. Poor Jake has developed some food allergies."

Molly felt a pang of worry at Chloe's countenance. "I take it you're not dating anymore."

Chloe spun her mug slowly on the table, her eyes on the marshmallow melting into the dark liquid. "We only went out three times, but I like him. He's funny and smart. And I thought he was a nice guy."

"But he did something that wasn't nice?"

"No, but it was confusing," Chloe said. "We went to a movie on our first date, then to a gallery opening the next time, and apple picking the last time. Nothing serious. I thought we were getting to be good friends, possibly something more. But then he suddenly called the clinic and told our receptionist that he was taking Jake to a new vet."

Molly gaped. "Did he give a reason?"

"No, which makes the whole thing much weirder," Chloe said. "I tried to call him, but he didn't return my call. I am not going to beg the man for an explanation, but it's left me confused. I thought we were having fun."

"And you can't think of any rough spots the last time you were out together?" Molly asked. "No arguments or weird reactions on his part to something you said? Sometimes people can be offended by things you never expected."

"That's the problem. We had a great time, and he seemed happy when the evening ended. He even suggested some upcoming events we might attend together, including something at his business. Then nothing." Chloe threw her hands in the air. "It doesn't make a speck of sense."

"I wish I had better advice, but this is probably one you'll need to write off."

"Probably," Chloe said, disappointment clear in her tone. "But I did hope we could be friends. It's rare to find a guy you can hang out with. Speaking of which, how's Fergus?"

Molly hoped her cheeks weren't as red as they felt at the mention of her handsome friend, Fergus MacGregor, who owned the Castleglen golf resort and lodge. They'd met when Molly had visited Loch Mallaig on family vacations in her youth, and they'd reconnected since she had moved to town. "He's as well as always." She raised her eyebrows. "In fact, we'll be having Thanksgiving dinner with him."

Chloe sat up straight. "Oh no, am I crashing plans?"

Molly laughed. "Not a bit. Fergus is hosting a special Thanksgiving dinner for his staff. He invited everyone from Bread on Arrival to attend since we provide the desserts and breads for the resort."

"That's kind of him," Chloe said. "Are you sure he won't mind me coming too?"

"I'll ask him, of course, but I'm sure he won't mind," Molly said. Fergus was nothing if not welcoming and generous. "Carol and Harvey passed since they'll be hosting their own family Thanksgiving, but Laura and I are going. I have no doubt Fergus will be glad to have you too."

"That sounds good. As long as it's not a date or anything."

"Nope. Fergus and I are just friends." As she said the words, Molly almost completely believed them. She and Fergus had known each other since childhood. Of course, Fergus had also been her first crush. But that was long ago, before they'd both grown up, married, and had families of their own. Now they were single again, but some foolish attempt at romance wasn't going to ruin their friendship, Molly was determined about that.

Chloe yawned widely, then clamped a hand over her mouth. "Sorry. It's been a long day of driving."

"Are you sure you don't want my bed?" Molly asked.

Chloe shook her head. "Only a little help getting the couch pulled out."

They made fast work of setting up the bed while Angus supervised. Molly retrieved a few extra pillows from her bedroom and set them on Chloe's bed. "I'm going to clean up the kitchen and head to bed myself."

"Don't forget your book," Chloe said sleepily.

"I think I'm done reading for the night," Molly said. "I'm hoping to sleep, after all. I'll be up early in the morning because of the bakery, but you should sleep as long as you want."

"Thanks, Mom," Chloe said before giving her a hug.

After holding on a little longer than usual, Molly released her and headed to the kitchen. She cleaned up quickly, then carried her novel to her room to get it off the table. On the way, she peeked into the sitting room and saw Angus had joined Chloe on the mattress and lay curled up at her side. Molly wasn't surprised, since Chloe had always had an amazing way with animals. Even when she was tiny, she had befriended shy dogs and grumpy cats that no one else could get near.

Molly carried her book into her room and set it beside the bed as she changed. She didn't intend to read any more of the eerie story, not even to find out what happened to the woman racing across the moors in the dark. She stuck to her decision, though her eye was drawn to the book several times. "No," she told herself firmly. "No more spooky reading for one night."

She climbed into bed and fell asleep almost immediately, only to find herself dreaming of the moors where she wandered in a long wool cape that dragged the ground and snagged constantly on brush. Though no one chased her, the annoyance with the cape only grew until suddenly she heard wild barking.

Molly sat up in bed. "Angus?" She scrambled out and found Angus and Chloe standing near the door to the interior stairs.

Chloe stared at her in confusion. "Are you expecting anyone?"

"I wasn't even expecting you," Molly said. "But if Angus thinks there's something we should check on, we'd best do it."

"Right." Chloe glanced around. "I don't suppose you have a baseball bat."

Molly shook her head. "We'll count on Angus to protect us. Besides, it's probably a raccoon in the trash cans."

Chloe bobbed her head. "Right. The quiet life in the country."

Molly opened the door and Angus rushed out, barking wildly as he raced down the stairs. Molly followed him with Chloe right behind her, her hand touching Molly's shoulder. When they reached the first floor and headed toward the back door, Angus kept up the barks of alarm.

"Mom," Chloe said anxiously. "I smell smoke."

Molly sniffed. "I do too."

They reached the back door. Molly flipped the locks and flung it open, only to be met by a wall of flames.

2

Molly and Chloe jumped back in shock, bumping into one another and nearly tripping over Angus, who had fortunately backed away from the door before Molly had opened it.

Molly quickly realized the inferno was contained to a bundle of corn shocks set in a metal bucket filled with bundled newspapers. The kitchen had a shiny fire extinguisher mounted on the wall and Molly quickly put out the flames, though the smell of smoke lingered around the doorway. The blaze had been alarming and potentially dangerous with so many dry leaves blowing around, but thankfully it hadn't had a chance to spread to anything.

With the force of the fire extinguisher's spray, the corn shocks crumpled down around the bucket, and Molly frowned at the sodden heap. "That was the display from our front porch. I guess this is someone's idea of a joke."

"I'm not laughing," Chloe replied as she knelt to examine the newspapers in the bucket. "Were these newspapers originally in the display?"

Molly shook her head. "Laura put miniature gourds around the base when she set it up. It was really cute."

"I'm sure it was." Chloe reached out to poke the mess and came up with a piece of charred string. "These papers were tied up."

Molly took the string from her. "That doesn't make much sense. I remember when your grandfather was teaching me how to set a campfire, he said you had to crumple paper because a bundle won't burn well. The oxygen can't get to all the pages."

"I guess the kids who set the fire could have used some lessons." Chloe rubbed at the char on her fingertips. "You should probably call the police."

"The police?"

"What if the flames had gotten high enough to reach the roof?" Chloe gestured to the small overhang above the door, then the fenced-in area where Angus loved playing in the dry autumn leaves. "And that's not far away. A single drifting ember could have set a fire. What if Angus had been out here?"

That wasn't likely in the middle of the night, but Molly understood her daughter's concern. "I suppose I should get a report on the record. It's possible this is part of a string of pranks. Kids get bored quickly in the cold months."

Angus came forward and snuffled at the burned papers, making himself sneeze in the process. Molly tugged him inside and closed the door.

Chloe scooped up Angus and snuggled him. "If you point me in the right direction, I'll put on coffee while you make the call. Judging from the way the sky is turning a little pink, I don't think we'll be going back to bed."

And that means this is going to be a long day. Molly showed Chloe the coffee setup, then headed for the phone. She already had the faint headache that signaled insufficient sleep, but hopefully coffee would help with that.

Soon Molly and Chloe were sipping coffee and staring out the front window of Bread on Arrival as they waited for the police to arrive. Behind them, Angus took advantage of one of his rare romps through the customer areas of the bakery, sniffing every chair leg with glee. Though Molly reminded herself over and over that the newspaper fire was surely a prank, she still didn't feel comfortable putting Angus upstairs where she couldn't see him. Not yet.

Chloe offered her mother a weak smile. "You sent me all the photos of the bakery, but it's even more impressive in person."

Molly knew Chloe was trying to distract them, but her gaze swept the customer area anyway. She loved the rustic, Northwoods-style furniture with rough Celtic knots carved into the chairbacks and on the braces. They always reminded her of the Scottish community where she had made her home. Some of the people were a bit rough around the edges as well, but extraordinary in their own way. "Sometimes I feel like we've always been here."

"I can imagine that." Chloe sipped her coffee, her eyes turning toward the shadowy street. "How are the police around here?"

"Kind," Molly said. "And competent. I almost wish I hadn't called, though. I'm not certain it's a police matter."

"I'm pretty sure it's something they'll want on record," Chloe insisted. "Though I suppose we may have been able to catch another hour of sleep if we hadn't bothered. Hopefully you can get a nap in later."

"Only ten hours to go until closing time." Molly groaned and smacked herself in the forehead. "I can't believe I forgot. It's Friday. Tonight is The Wandering."

"The Wandering? Is that a play or something?"

Molly shook her head. "It's a community event, a kind of progressive dinner hosted by different businesses around town. It celebrates the movement of Scots to Loch Mallaig. Well, to America really, but mostly to Loch Mallaig."

"Sounds nice. Are you going to go?"

"In a way. Bread on Arrival is the last stop. We're going to serve hot beverages and small dessert nibbles. The plan is to have them out on the porch since the weather is unseasonably warm." She grimaced, thinking about the hole left by the now-charred corn shocks.

Chloe gaped at her. "This is warm?"

"You grew up in Chicago and work in Milwaukee," Molly teased. "I thought I raised you to think any weather that doesn't freeze your nose off is warm."

"I work indoors mostly," Chloe said. "Though I feel for the large-animal vets. I'd freeze to death in some of the weather they take in stride."

Chloe and Molly perked up as a Loch Mallaig police car parked in front of the shop. Officer Greer Anderson got out of the car and waved at them as she headed toward the bakery door. The blonde, thirtysomething officer was petite, but with her athletic build and confident manner, there weren't many people Greer couldn't handle.

Molly was glad to see her. They played together in a bagpiping group, The Piping Yoopers, and they'd become friends. She knew Greer wouldn't scold her for calling the police over a silly prank. In fact, Greer often scolded her when she didn't call over minor things.

Molly opened the door as Greer reached it. "Sorry to get you out this early."

"Don't be sorry," Greer said. "I was on duty, catching up on paperwork, which is the bane of my existence. You saved me." She sniffed. "At least you can't smell the fire in here." She thrust out her hand toward Chloe. "You must be Chloe. I'm Greer Anderson."

Chloe shook her hand. "Pleased to meet you. I had to twist Mom's arm to get her to call."

Greer smiled wryly at Molly. "I'm shocked." She rubbed her hands together. "Let's go examine the evidence."

"It's out back." Molly led the way to the rear entrance and opened the door.

After donning gloves, the officer squatted to study the mess carefully. She even lifted a newspaper bundle to sniff it. "I think some kind of accelerant was poured on these. I'm guessing paraffin. With an accelerant, this would have burned hot. You're lucky you caught it before it could spread." She stood and studied Molly. "Annoyed anyone lately?"

Molly shook her head. "Not as far as I'm aware. I figured this was some kind of prank."

Greer stared at the jumble of papers and corn shocks. "It's a little early for the teens around here to be getting cabin fever. I'll take some samples, but there isn't much more I can do."

"I didn't expect you to do anything about it," Molly said. "But I figured you may want to see it in case this is the beginning of a trend."

Greer grinned at her. "Spoken like a true investigator."

Chloe, who'd been unusually quiet since they'd reached the back door, yawned widely, then grimaced apologetically. "Phew, sorry. Mom, if you don't need me, I think I'll take Angus up and sleep some more. If there's going to be an event tonight, I need a nap."

Molly patted Chloe's arm. "Go ahead and take the bed. Flip the latch on the doggie door in the office before you settle down. That way Angus can let himself out if he needs to."

"You got it." Chloe tipped her head at Greer. "Nice to meet you."

Greer had knelt down to collect her sample and waved at Chloe with the evidence bag. "You too." Once Chloe was gone, Greer stood and tucked the evidence bag in her pocket. "Is there any chance someone could be playing a prank on Chloe?"

Molly shook her head. "She only got here last night after supper."

"I see. Well, let me snap some pictures of this, and I'll be on my way. Once I get a report written up, I'll drop by for you to read and sign it."

After Greer left, Molly retreated to the kitchen. She was pondering how to clean up the soggy, charred mess without getting it all over herself when Carol and Laura arrived to get started on the morning's tasks before opening the bakery. Alarmed by the mess out back, they immediately demanded an explanation. They listened with concern as Molly explained about all the excitement they'd missed, including Chloe's arrival and the burning corn shocks.

"How terrible," Carol said with a shudder after Molly described the scene. "Sounds like a burning effigy."

"Now that you say that, it was pretty gruesome." Molly grimaced. "I still haven't figured out how to clean it up without wearing it."

"Leave it for Hamish," Laura suggested. "His feelings would be hurt if you didn't, and he'll have an exact strategy to take care of it."

"And it'll be the right strategy," Carol added. "As it always is."

The three women laughed. Hamish Bruce was a dear friend and a huge help at the bakery, but he was also prone to thinking his way of doing things was the only one.

Laura pulled slips of paper from her pocket. "We don't have time for cleanup anyway. With The Wandering tonight, it's going to be a busy day. I made to-do lists for everyone."

Usually the partner with the plan, ever-organized Carol raised an eyebrow, but took her list and nodded approval as she read it. Molly didn't mind being told what she should do. After the limited sleep she'd had, she would probably need a lot of direction.

They were equal partners at Bread on Arrival and dear enough friends that they mostly made room for each person's idiosyncrasies. Laura had previously been the head chef at a trendy NYC restaurant, but she'd left the frenzied pace and late nights behind for early mornings whipping up shortbread and Selkirk bannock. Carol, a retired high school math teacher, had made wedding cakes on the side for years, and she brought both her baking talents and her knack for organizing to the bakehouse. Since Molly's background was event planning, she bowed to both of her other partners when it came to baking, and focused more on marketing the bakehouse and serving up smiles in the front of the house. As she read through the list Laura had made her, she was glad to see that today's tasks were fairly disaster proof. It was as if her friend had known she'd be a zombie today.

"I had a thought," Carol said as she began gathering ingredients to mix up a batch of buttercream frosting. "I wonder if the fire on the doorstep could be about The Wandering."

Molly cocked her head in surprise. "Why would it be?"

"Some people don't appreciate opportunity," Laura said as she opened one of the coolers to grab the carton of heavy cream for scones.

"What are you talking about?" Molly asked.

Carol grabbed a wrapped brick of butter and took it to her station. "This is why you shouldn't have skipped out on the planning meeting. It was a rowdy one since not every business owner in town thought The Wandering was a good idea."

"Oh?" Molly was surprised. "This is the first I've heard about it. Usually everyone around here is gung ho for community events, especially those that celebrate our Scottish heritage."

"You should have heard Grizela Duff." Laura launched into a brogue. "'The history of the Scots in America is sacred and not to be used to peddle sausages and cider!'"

That did sound like something the feisty librarian would say, and Molly wondered if Grizela's annoyance at Bread on Arrival explained her recommendation of the book that had scared Molly senseless. But it didn't explain the prank. "It's not like Grizela would have burned corn shocks in effigy on our back stoop. That's not exactly her style."

"But Grizela isn't the only one annoyed," Carol said. "She got the entire historical society fired up about it."

"I don't see the problem," Laura put in. "The timing of The Wandering gives businesses a chance to showcase different Scottish-inspired specialty foods or beverages. We hope customers will think of us as a place to buy delicious bread and desserts for upcoming holiday dinners, but how does that sully the Scots?"

Molly didn't know, but if there actually was some feud over the event, it could make the evening interesting. Since there was nothing for it but to take the occasion as it came, she focused on the list in her hand and got to work.

Surprisingly, Chloe didn't come down all morning. Molly knew her daughter was tired, but Chloe had always considered Laura and Carol to be family, and Molly kept expecting her to show up in the kitchen to hang out with them as they worked. By lunchtime, Molly was actively concerned, so she slipped upstairs.

A refrigerator magnet held a note from Chloe explaining that she was window-shopping with Angus. *I didn't want to get in the way downstairs. Everyone must be busy with the event tonight. Please tell Carol and Laura that I'll pitch in when I get back. I'm not a baker, but I can wash dishes or cut brownies. Or be a taste tester!*

Molly chuckled. At least she knew Chloe was okay. Molly drew a quick heart on the bottom of the note and went downstairs, feeling relieved and able to focus on the new to-do list Laura handed her at the base of the steps.

Molly glanced over the list, then joined Carol in filling mini tarts for The Wandering. As she scooped delicious-smelling apricot filling into the tarts, she noticed Carol staring at her. "What?"

"You're clearly exhausted," Carol said. Molly knew she was serious when she used her no-nonsense tone, perfected over years of teaching boisterous teenagers. "We could probably manage for a while if you want to run up and take a power nap. Sometimes even a short snooze makes a world of difference."

"I suspect if I put my head down, you wouldn't see me again before dark," Molly told her. She gently bumped shoulders with her old friend. "Thank you for the offer, but I'm fine. I'll be glad to get to bed tonight, though."

Carol peered at her for another moment, then relaxed the tight line of her mouth. "If you say so, but remember we're not all twenty anymore. Losing sleep hurts more now."

Don't I know it. But Molly only smiled and focused on the tarts. The next few hours blurred as she moved from one task to the next, staying busy enough that her weariness never had a chance to catch up with her.

When Molly walked to the front of the bakery to grab another cup of coffee, she found their part-time employee Bridget Ross as bright and cheery as always. Molly marveled at Bridget's bottomless well of energy. *Of course, she is nineteen.* Then Molly gave herself a mental shake. *What is it with me and age today?*

"Something wrong?" Bridget whispered as she joined Molly at the coffee station. "I heard about the fire. Are you okay?"

"I'm fine. A little tired."

"I bet," Bridget said sympathetically. She snapped her fingers. "Oh, someone came by asking for your daughter earlier."

Molly lifted her eyebrows in surprise. How many people could possibly know Chloe was in town? "Who?"

"I didn't know her, and she didn't give her name. Honestly, I didn't immediately recognize the name Chloe." Bridget's cheeks pinked as she spoke, nearly matching the raspberry streak in her glossy black hair. "We were busy, and I wasn't thinking. Anyway, I told the woman that no one named Chloe worked here."

"That's odd. I didn't think Chloe knew anyone around here." Molly considered the possibilities. "Maybe it's someone she met while shopping this morning. She tends to make friends wherever she goes."

"When I meet Chloe, I'll be sure to let her know I'm sorry for telling the woman she wasn't here."

"She wasn't here," Molly said. "She's been out shopping. What did the woman look like?"

"Tall, sharp features, expensive clothes. Oh, excuse me. I'm needed." Bridget hurried away to wait on a customer who had just arrived at the counter, leaving Molly by the coffee station.

Molly sipped her coffee and observed the bakery, enjoying the view as she always did. Most of the tables and chairs were empty since they were near closing time. The few customers who remained were seated near the stone fireplace where the room was warmest, which made Molly suspect the temperature must be dropping outside. Though it was barely three o'clock, the window showed a world slipping quietly toward dusk. It wasn't dark by any means, but neither was it the bright, clear day they'd enjoyed earlier.

"Tonight should be fun," Bridget said once her customer had been served. "Thanks for letting me go on The Wandering."

Molly waved dismissively. "Of course."

"Neeps and Tatties is the last stop before we come here," Bridget went on, referring to the wonderful Scottish restaurant across the street from Bread on Arrival. "I'll only stay there a few minutes so I can be over here before the crowd."

"Don't feel you have to rush. Hamish should be here right around closing. We'd appreciate your help with serving, but I think we have setup covered."

Bridget beamed at her. "I have the best bosses in the world."

Molly appreciated the young woman's enthusiasm and managed a grin of her own before she headed into the kitchen. Carol was rolling Scottish snowballs in coconut while Laura was moving melting moments cookies from a pan to the cooling rack. Their dessert selection was going to be simple, leaning toward handheld desserts so they could avoid a crowd of visitors wondering what to do with a plate when they finished.

"Everyone has clustered around the fireplace out in the café," Molly told her partners. "Do you think it's warm enough for us to serve on the porch?"

"I checked a few minutes ago when I was rearranging our front porch display," Laura said. "It is cold, but we'll be serving hot coffee, cider, and cocoa. And the customer area will be open to anyone who wants to warm up by the fire."

"Ourselves included," Carol said with a slight shiver. "I do not enjoy the cold."

"Even though you're the one who keeps chickens," Molly reminded her. "A hobby that puts you outside every day of the year."

"On the frozen days, I can usually talk Harvey into doing the chicken chores."

Before Molly could respond, Chloe bounded into the kitchen. "I'm home!"

Carol and Laura both abandoned their desserts to hug Chloe, fussing over her like family. Chloe's fair coloring, a trait she'd inherited from Molly, tended to show exhaustion clearly, and Molly was glad to see that Chloe's nap had eased the dark circles under her eyes.

"Did you get some holiday shopping done?" Molly asked.

"A little, but I was mostly admiring," Chloe said. "I enjoyed watching Angus charm everyone we met. He's quite a little celebrity around here. You wouldn't believe how many people recognized him."

"Angus does tend to make an impression," Carol said with a chuckle.

"I put the star upstairs so he can recover from greeting his adoring public." Chloe glanced around the kitchen, then grabbed an apron from a nearby hook. "So how can I help?"

Laura assigned Chloe a few simple tasks, and soon they were all working together to prep treats for serving.

Bridget popped her head in just after closing time. "The door is locked," she announced. "I just need to change clothes for tonight. I brought the cutest outfit."

"Bridget, have you met Chloe?" Molly asked.

"I introduced myself on the way in," Chloe answered.

"Oh good." Molly gestured toward the ceiling. "Bridget, you can use my apartment to change if you want."

With a chipper thank-you, Bridget popped back out of the kitchen. Turning back to the preparations underway, Molly was pleased to see they were nearly done. She could almost believe she would have time to sneak off for a quick nap before everyone arrived.

Then the back door slammed and heavy footsteps thudded toward the kitchen. "What is that mess outside?" Hamish demanded as he stomped into the kitchen.

Molly realized she'd totally forgotten about the charred corn shocks and sodden newspapers. "Someone's idea of a joke, I imagine," she explained. "I completely forgot about the bucket. Would you be able to clean it up?"

"Aye," Hamish said. "The bucket'll take me only a minute, but what do you intend to do about the paint?"

"Paint!" Molly, Laura, and Carol yelped in unison.

"What are you talking about?" Laura asked.

Hamish's lips quirked dourly beneath his snow-white beard. "You best come and see."

They all hurried outside to the yard, then turned to view the house. Someone had thrown bright red paint on the creamy yellow siding near the back door. It ran down the wall, looking horrifically like blood. A puddle had formed near the sooty bucket of newspapers, and someone had dipped into one of the red pools to write a missive on the stoop. *Stop now!*

Molly stared at the carnage, her hand at her throat, barely believing what she was seeing. Who could be so angry with them? "Stop what?" she whispered. "The Wandering?"

"We don't have that kind of power," Laura said.

"Perhaps someone thinks we do," Carol said, one eyebrow raised in apprehension. "And they seem to be eager to get us to use it."

3

Molly was grateful when Greer Anderson showed up after they called the police.

"Do you think it's another prank?" Carol asked after the officer had seen the red paint and taken photos and samples.

"If this was the only incident, I'd say yes," Greer answered. "But on top of the fire, it suggests someone has a problem with you, and they could be escalating."

At the word *escalating*, Molly shivered. That suggested they were going to see more vandalism, and they'd already had too much. "What can we do about it?"

Greer studied the paint. "Power washing should take most of it off. It's still wet."

"I think Molly was asking what we should do to stop this person," Laura explained.

"With two incidents, I'm sure the chief will authorize frequent drive-bys of the bakery," Greer answered. "Though the fact that this was done in broad daylight suggests the culprit has no shortage of nerve." She closed her notebook and shoved it in her pocket. "You should try to figure out who you've upset recently."

After the officer left, Hamish stepped forward. "My power washer's in the shop, but my friend Kelvin Mooney's got every gadget known to man," he said. "Loves to use them too. I can call him to come clean up this mess."

"Do you think he can fix this?" Carol asked skeptically.

"Kelvin's done wonders with paint spills," Hamish said. "There was one time Brent Overbee's cows got out of the paddock—"

Laura held up a hand to ward off one of Hamish's classic tales. "You can tell us about the cows later. For now, please call your friend. We have to get the prep finished before customers start arriving." She clapped her hands. "Remember, no one will want to see long faces when they get here."

So they returned to work. The catastrophe outside had thrown them off of Laura's carefully planned schedule, but with Chloe's help they caught up in no time. Molly noticed Chloe casting worried glances toward the back door more than once. In the past, Chloe had complained that Loch Mallaig was dangerous despite the quiet setting, since Molly and her friends sometimes found themselves in these situations. *It's not as if we* try *to get wrapped up in mysteries,* Molly argued silently. *They just sort of find us.* Though now that she thought about it, that logic seemed to prove Chloe's point rather than hers.

Finally, they had everything ready for The Wandering visitors. Before heading upstairs to freshen up, Chloe walked to the front of the bakery. "Whoa!" she crowed. "You guys should come see this."

The Bread on Arrival partners joined her at the front window and watched the Neeps and Tatties parking lot fill to bursting. Crowds of people hurried into the restaurant.

"Do you think those are all Wanderers?" Molly asked.

"They must be," Laura said. "The restaurant is popular, but I've never seen it overrun quite like that, and with everyone showing up all at the same time."

"I hope we have enough food," Carol said as they continued to gape at the crowd.

"If we start to run out, we'll pull from the cookies we have for tomorrow," Laura answered briskly. "We can always come in early to make up for it."

Molly suppressed a groan at the thought of an extra-early day on top of her present weariness. "At least The Wandering appears to be a big success."

"Which means we have to do this every year," Hamish said grumpily as he joined them. "Kelvin is here to clean up the back porch. He says the paint should be tacky enough to remove it completely. Seems we were saved by the damp air."

"Nice to have some reason to rejoice in cold, damp weather," Carol replied.

"Let's get set up outside," Laura said. Molly was amused by her brisk tone, thinking it must have been interesting to work in her kitchen when she was a head chef in New York.

A few minutes later, Molly carried a tray of mini tarts out to the porch while Chloe followed her with two baskets, one piled with melting moments and the other full of Scottish snowballs. Laura was already on the porch arranging the hot beverage station, which would serve cinnamon hot chocolate, spiced cider, and decaf coffee to the Wanderers. Molly suspected that would be a popular station since the dropping temperatures and moisture in the air made it decidedly nippy, even with her cozy jacket on.

"I'm going to take Angus for a walk before everyone gets here," Chloe said as she set the basket on the table. "He's going to feel abandoned when he hears all the people down here that he can't get to."

"That's kind of you," Molly said. "Just be sure to keep him out of the way of Hamish's friend while he's cleaning up the back door."

"I will," Chloe sang out before trotting inside.

Molly was glad that her daughter had apparently gotten over the fretting she'd been doing earlier. *Or the fretting I thought she'd been doing.* Molly had to admit she sometimes worried about her only child a little too much. Chloe was perfectly fine.

Laura frowned toward the food table. "Molly, could you ask Carol to whip up another batch of melting moments? They might spread a little since we can't chill the dough, but I think it would be good to have one more batch."

"You don't want to borrow from tomorrow's cookies?"

"I'd rather avoid dipping into those if we can. I hadn't considered that we might have a late night tonight."

"Right." Molly hurried in and found Carol handing Hamish a tray of tarts to carry to the table.

"Laura asked if you'd make a batch of melting moments," Molly said. "I think she's getting nervous about the crowd too."

"No problem," Carol agreed quickly. "It's an easy recipe."

"Want me to help?"

"Sure. Grab some butter from the cooler, please."

"Happy to oblige." Molly typically limited her baking tasks, as she knew she didn't have Carol or Laura's skills with pastry or decorating. Her friends often told her that she was too hard on herself, but Molly felt their customers deserved the best possible baked goods, and she didn't make them. At least she could gather ingredients.

Carol coaxed Molly into whipping up a second batch of melting moments right alongside her. Under her friend's watchful eye, Molly gave it a try, and before she knew it, they were pulling perfect cookies from the oven.

"I'll carry these out," Molly said after they'd filled a basket. "Then I'll offer to man the table so Laura can come in from the cold for a few minutes before the crowd arrives."

"Good plan," Carol said. "Once the Wanderers arrive, I'll watch over everyone in the customer area and clean up where needed."

Outside, Laura gratefully accepted Molly's offer to take over her chilly job. "I can't feel my toes," she whispered.

"Go stand by the fire a bit," Molly said. "That should warm you up."

Laura slipped inside as Bridget rushed up the front steps, her eyes wide. "Everyone will be here soon. The crowd is enormous."

"You can take over the beverage table until Laura comes out," Molly said. "The hot pots should help keep you from freezing. I'll be on the pastry table."

Bridget gave her a cheery salute and slipped behind the table as Molly peered out into the night and saw the first of the Wanderers crossing the street. They were laughing and chattering as they queued up at the tables.

Molly beamed at the group waiting for their desserts. The first to step up to the table was a distinguished man who wore a suit under his long coat. He had an athletic build and dark hair, going gray at the temples. Molly was certain she would have remembered him if she'd met him before. "Good evening," she said. "I hope you're enjoying The Wandering."

"It's been interesting," he said. "I was lucky to come to town in time to check it out."

As he picked a tart for his dessert, Molly gave herself a mental pat on the back for being right about the man being a stranger to Loch Mallaig. Since the line behind the man was long, Molly didn't engage him in more conversation. The next man in line was a stranger too, but with a decidedly different appearance. He was hefty and considerably shorter, dressed in jeans and a thick jacket. He surveyed the table of treats avidly.

"Could I have two, please?" he asked. "I missed the beginning of the food, and I'm hungry."

"As long as one choice is a melting moment," Molly said. "We made extras of those."

"Thank you," the man said gratefully, then grabbed a tart and a cookie. He moved along to the beverage table, where he said something to the well-dressed stranger and they both chuckled.

At least people are having fun. Molly found herself smiling a little brighter as the next person stepped up.

Her smile froze around the edges as she recognized Wilma Guthrie, the police department receptionist. Wilma was hard to miss with her bright red hair, teased into a wild disarray that would have made any 1980s TV star proud. Wilma was an incurable gossip whose job put her in the perfect position to hear, or mishear, all sorts of news.

As Molly expected, Wilma stage-whispered loudly as she picked up a tart, "I heard about your vandalism problem. The teenagers are getting out of hand, in my opinion."

"We don't know who splashed the paint," Molly said. "But it's being taken care of." She hoped Wilma would accept that and move on. Molly didn't appreciate the curious gazes the redhead was drawing.

Wilma narrowed her eyes at Molly. "You sure you haven't upset anyone? You tend to do that."

I do not! Molly forced a pleasant expression. "Not lately." She pointedly turned her attention to the Wanderer behind Wilma. "What can I get you tonight?"

Taking the dismissal in good grace, Wilma headed for the hot beverage table. Molly hoped Wilma wouldn't grill Bridget too.

At the sound of raised voices near the street, Molly rose up on her toes to peer around the line of Wanderers. Grizela Duff stood at the edge of the bakery property, barely lit by the parking lot lights of Neeps and Tatties across the street. She was flanked by a few others from the Loch Mallaig Historical Society and a couple of teenagers who were an unexpected addition to the group. Even in the dark, Molly recognized the slumped shoulders and shuffling feet of people who did not want to be there.

"This event is an insult to our heritage!" Grizela shouted, her voice carried all the command that she normally used to shame chatty library patrons.

To Molly's relief, Hamish headed toward the group. Usually he wouldn't have been her first choice to defuse a situation, but he and Grizela seemed to be cut from similar cloth—or tartan. "Now, now, there's no insult here," he said, in what he must have deemed a soothing tone. "Only cookies and tarts."

Whatever Grizela said next was less clear, though her posture remained belligerent. Molly decided to focus on the customers in front of her and hope Hamish would manage to calm instead of incite the crowd. With Hamish, things could go either way.

Carol walked out of the bakery and down the stairs with enough vigor to make Molly hope that her levelheaded friend would settle things. Passing Carol on her way, Chloe climbed the porch steps with Angus right on her heels, then slipped behind the table to join Molly. Angus flopped down between them.

"You've worn Angus out," Molly said as she handed a customer a tart nestled in wax paper.

"He'll sleep well tonight," Chloe said, then focused on the line of customers. "Who's next?"

The line quickly divided in two and Chloe worked alongside her mother. Not only was it warmer with another body beside her and a little Scottie sprawled over her feet, but it was a joy to see Chloe interacting with the customers. She had a warm, generous manner that must be a huge help to her veterinary practice.

When the line was finally done, Chloe leaned close to Molly and whispered, "Okay, the curiosity is killing me. What's with the picket line? I never thought I'd see protesters here."

"They aren't mad at us, specifically," Molly said. "Grizela didn't want the town to have The Wandering. She thinks it's too commercial. The rest of the people are part of the historical society with Grizela, but I think she made them come."

"They don't seem to be nearly as passionate about it as she is," Chloe said. "And did you see that a couple of them sneaked up to get hot beverages?"

"I didn't see that," Molly said, amused. "You multitask better than me, if you could keep up with customers and watch the protesters at the same time."

"It's a gift," Chloe replied lightly. "The grumpy lady did not get a hot drink. Though she was steamed."

Molly chuckled at the joke. "Grizela tends to get worked up when she doesn't get her way." She glanced toward the street, wondering if Hamish had made any progress.

Grizela hadn't budged from her spot on the sidewalk. Though Carol had given up, Hamish continued to argue with the librarian, but their voices didn't carry. Finally, Hamish threw his hands in the air and walked away. Grizela watched him go, her arms still crossed.

"Mom," Chloe said. "Do you think she could have set the fire and thrown the paint? She was mad enough."

"No, that's not Grizela's sort of thing," Molly insisted. Grizela hadn't always been completely innocent when she found a cause she felt was important, but the librarian would have no reason to target the bakery specifically . . . would she?

"What's not her sort of thing?" Hamish asked, having caught Molly's remark when he came over to get a cookie. "Because being reasonable is not her sort of thing."

Molly felt a smile tug at the corners of her mouth. *And that would be the pot calling the kettle black, now wouldn't it?*

"Do you have any idea who would have set the fire and thrown the paint, Mr. Bruce?" Chloe asked.

"Certainly not Grizela," Hamish said in a tone that suggested he'd brook no argument on that. "I'm sure it was high school kids. It's always the same when the weather is cold and the days are short. I think it brings out the mischief." He scowled. "You couldn't believe some of the pranks my students pulled."

He launched into a recollection of one prank from his days teaching high school history that had involved a donkey and the principal's hat and tie, but Molly's attention wandered to the dark lawn. If there had been only one incident, she'd have accepted the thought of a prank in an instant, but two events in such close succession? That felt like a grudge to her. She only hoped that whoever was holding the grudge felt they'd done enough.

Molly shivered. Whether it was from cold or worry, she couldn't have said.

4

At long last, the porch was empty of Wanderers, though a few holdouts were chatting and sipping cider and cocoa next to the fireplace inside. Molly figured they were putting off heading out into the chilly night as long as possible. She and Chloe began cleaning up the serving table while Laura and Carol worked on the beverage station.

"Hamish and Bridget, could you go inside to gently encourage people to finish up?" Laura asked. She gave Hamish a meaningful look. "Gently."

Hamish puffed up. "When am I ever anything but the soul of kindness?"

Bridget laughed brightly and tugged on Hamish's thick wool sweater. "Come show me."

As the door closed behind Hamish and Bridget, a voice sang out from the shadows near the steps. "Am I too late?"

A woman started up the stairs. Her rounded face appeared first out of the darkness, her pale skin nearly glowing in the low light while her coal-black hair seemed to carry the shadows with her.

"I'm sorry I'm late, but I couldn't get away from work," she said. "I wanted to taste some of the special Bread on Arrival treats I've heard about."

"Come right over," Molly told her. "We're out of tarts, but we have plenty of melting moments."

"You're also welcome to hot cocoa or cider," Laura added. "If you want coffee, I can go inside and get a cup. This urn is empty."

"Hot cocoa would be wonderful." The woman blew on her fingers. "It's freezing out."

"You must be new to town," Carol said as she handed over a foam cup of cocoa. "Or terribly busy, if you haven't been able to come to Bread on Arrival until now."

"It's a little of both." The woman took a sip of the cocoa, then added, "I work at the Two Scots Guesthouse."

"Oh, that's a lovely place," Molly said. "The owners are so nice." Then Molly thought of something the woman had said about wanting to taste Bread on Arrival treats. The bakery supplied bread and pastries to the guesthouse. Why hadn't this woman tasted any of them?

"That they are," the woman said, pulling Molly out of her own thoughts. The stranger walked to the dessert table and picked up one of the cookies. Then she studied Molly and Chloe curiously. "You two look alike. Mother and daughter?"

"That's right," Molly said, introducing herself and Chloe.

"Pleased to meet you. My name is Georgia Pinter."

Laura and Carol piped up with their names as well, then Chloe asked, "Are you enjoying Loch Mallaig? I'm new too."

"It's lovely. Everyone is friendly and kind." The latecomer focused intently on Chloe as she spoke—so intently that Molly was almost uncomfortable with it.

"Feel free to take a second cookie," Molly said, pulling the woman's attention away from her daughter. "We're cleaning up, but please don't feel rushed." She hated to acknowledge it, even to herself, but she'd feel a bit better if the woman would leave. Something about her piercing gaze was making Molly nervous.

Though Molly had spoken, the woman barely gave her a glance as she chatted with Chloe. Molly continued to clean up the table, but she listened closely to the conversation. Nothing about it was odd.

The woman talked about shops she had visited in Loch Mallaig, and Chloe chimed in with some of the ones she'd been in earlier. Molly gave herself a mental shake for being silly. It was nice seeing Chloe making friends.

The woman seemed to take the hint when Laura and Carol started carrying urns into the bakery. Chloe excused herself and rushed to help while Molly covered the trays of remaining treats.

"I suppose I should go," Georgia said. "I have to work early in the morning." She chuckled. "I guess that's a challenge you have experience with."

"Some," Molly agreed and was relieved when the woman bid her good night and left. As she carried the trays of food inside, she suddenly remembered the woman Bridget had mentioned earlier who had come looking for Chloe. She recalled Bridget saying the woman had sharp features. It couldn't have been Georgia, whose edges were all rounded. Molly shook her head. Why would she think it was? Georgia clearly had never met Chloe before.

When Molly got to the kitchen with her trays, she found Chloe washing out one of the urns. She told her about the woman who had stopped at the bakery asking for her. "Bridget said she had sharp features and was well-dressed."

Chloe shrugged. "I met a couple people who fit that description when I was shopping. The people in Loch Mallaig are friendly." She pulled a face. "Well, except for the grumpy librarian. I don't think I'd ever have the nerve to check out a book here."

"If you did, you wouldn't bring it in late."

Chloe giggled. "I wouldn't dare!"

On Saturday morning, Molly trotted downstairs to a kitchen already fragrant with festive baking aromas. Before she slipped into the kitchen, she went out the back door to check on the paint cleanup. They'd all checked before locking up the night before, but Molly wanted to see the area by the light of day. She found a stranger kneeling on the porch with a can of paint.

"*Guid mornin*!" he greeted her. "Are you one of the three Scottish hens?"

Molly resisted the urge to frown. She did not want her father's old nickname for Carol, Laura, and herself to get around, but that's probably what they got for sharing it with Hamish. "You must be Hamish's friend. Kelvin, right?" She examined the area where the paint had hit and was pleased to see it was remarkably clear of any red remains. "You're doing a fine job."

"Thanks. Luckily it was still pretty wet when I got to it." He waved his paintbrush. "I came this morning to touch up anything I missed yesterday."

"Wonderful, thank you. I appreciate you working so quickly."

"I'll take any excuse to fire up ol' Bessie," Kelvin said with a chuckle, apparently referring to his power washer.

Molly thanked him again, then went to the kitchen. She'd slept like the dead and didn't remember hearing her alarm, though she must have shut it off in her sleep. Normally Angus would have woken her, but he'd slept with Chloe again. She felt guilty for oversleeping, but her head was considerably clearer than it had been all day on Friday.

"Sorry I'm late," Molly said to Carol and Laura. She gestured over her shoulder with her thumb. "The porch looks good."

Laura paused in cutting a puffy blob of dough into dinner roll-size pieces. "Thankfully. And don't worry about being late. You must have needed the sleep."

"It's good to see you without dark smudges under your eyes," Carol added. She handed Molly a shaker of coarse sugar. "If you'll take over sprinkling these cookies and pop them in the oven, I can move on to putting together some chocolate cake batter."

"No problem." Molly appreciated it when she could take on a nice foolproof task. "How are you both doing?"

"I'm dealing with constant chaos," Carol moaned theatrically. "We kept the grandkids last night after The Wandering. I woke up to Maisie and Gavin arguing about which of their paper-bag turkeys were going to be the centerpiece for Thanksgiving dinner. When I got to them, they'd begun swatting one another with the turkeys."

Laura laughed. "That must have been hard on the turkeys."

"Catastrophic," Carol confirmed. "That's the one problem with twins. They have the same craft projects at the same time."

"I remember Chloe's paper-bag turkeys when she was little," Molly said as she sprinkled cookies. "But at least I only had one lopsided turkey to deal with."

Laura raised an eyebrow at Carol. "So, Solomon, how are you going to solve the problem of the turkeys?"

"Twin turkeys of course," Carol said. "Assuming anyone can tell the critters are turkeys anymore. The twins can create some impressive destruction. I left them giving their creations some first aid."

"Wise choice," Molly agreed.

"We'll crowd the food a tad," Carol said. "But I won't have any sad grandkids at my table."

As Molly finished sprinkling the pans of cookies and loaded them into the oven, she thought about how nice it would be to have a house full of grandchildren at holiday time. She supported Chloe's focus on her career, but she had to admit that sometimes Carol's stories made her a little wistful.

Around midmorning, Chloe came downstairs with Angus leashed and trailing her. She paused in the kitchen door to wish everyone a good morning. "I'm going to take Angus for a walk," she said. "But I promise not to disappear all day. As soon as I get back, I'll pitch in."

"No rush," Molly said. "You're technically on vacation."

"Chloe, hold on." Bridget had appeared at the door carrying a hefty arrangement of autumn-hued flowers. "These came for you."

"For me?" Chloe blinked. "Really?"

Molly peered at the dahlias, lilies, and mums. "Is there a card?"

"You been holding out on us?" Laura asked. "If you've got a boyfriend, we want all the details."

"One thing is clear," Carol put in. "He's well off."

Chloe found a card hidden among the blooms. She slipped it from the tiny envelope, then stared at it, her expression baffled. "They're from Camden Landry." She waved the card at her mother. "He's the guy I told you about, the one I went out with a couple of times."

Molly folded her arms over her chest. "The one who made you look bad at work? I hope he doesn't think you'd go out with him again."

"I can't imagine what he thinks," Chloe said.

"He was obviously a dolt," Carol said. "Maybe he grew a brain and realized it."

Chloe sighed deeply. "Is there a place I can leave the flowers down here? I want to take Angus for the walk I promised."

Molly figured Chloe also wanted some time to herself. "I'm sure we can find a place."

"We can put the flowers on top of one of the displays in the customer area," Carol suggested. "Let everyone enjoy them."

"Sounds good." Chloe tugged Angus to the back door.

When Chloe was gone and Bridget had returned to the front with the flowers, Molly pursed her lips. "I wonder how the man knew where to find Chloe."

"He could have called the clinic," Laura said. "And someone told him Chloe was going to her mother's. What if Chloe told him about her mother's bakery in the middle of nowhere?"

Molly wasn't sure Bread on Arrival would be part of Chloe's dating conversation, and she saw another flaw in that theory. "The clinic is closed for the bat removal."

"There could still be someone there," Carol said. "Or they could be forwarding calls to personal cell phones until the clinic reopens."

That was possible, but Carol's reasoning did nothing to assuage Molly's nerves. There was way too much weirdness going around. "I'm going to grab a coffee, and then I have some online orders to pack," she said. "Anyone else want coffee?"

"No thanks," Laura and Carol replied, virtually in unison.

Molly walked out to the customer area. Her eye went immediately to the elaborate flowers, then beyond them to the front window. She spotted Chloe and Angus outside on the front lawn. Angus trotted beside Chloe, his nose dipping now and then to sniff the grass enthusiastically. Each time, Chloe paused to let Angus have his way.

Chloe looked up suddenly, her attention on Neeps and Tatties. She raised a hand in greeting and headed for the street, clearly intending to cross. Molly surveyed the restaurant's parking lot, wondering who had called to Chloe. There were a handful of people, either heading into the restaurant or leaving. It wasn't surprising, as Neeps and Tatties served a great Scottish breakfast on the weekends. But Molly didn't see anyone who would have a reason to call to Chloe.

Her attention was tuned to the people in the parking lot, and she didn't immediately notice the dark SUV that was driving entirely too fast as it rushed out of the lot. To Molly's horror, the vehicle rushed into the street as Chloe and Angus were crossing, and it showed no sign of slowing down.

The huge vehicle barreled straight for Molly's precious daughter.

5

"Chloe!" Molly screamed, though there was no way her daughter could possibly hear her. Everyone in the bakehouse rushed to the window while Molly ran for the door.

She hadn't even reached the door when she saw the SUV barrel away down the road. For an instant, Molly was sure the vehicle must have hit either Chloe or Angus, but when the SUV was gone, she saw Chloe staring after it in horror for a second before scooping Angus up in her arms. The little dog and her daughter appeared fine.

Molly was nearly in tears when she got outside. "Chloe! Are you all right?"

Chloe checked the traffic carefully, then crossed over to her mom, clutching Angus in her arms and shaking from head to toe. The little dog licked her chin. "Did you see that? I felt the rearview mirror brush my jacket. He must have seen me."

"It was a man driving?" Molly asked.

Chloe stared at Molly for a moment without speaking, then shook her head. "I can't be sure. I don't think I saw the driver. It happened fast."

Molly ran through her own recall. She'd gotten an impression of a figure, though she couldn't recall any of its features, having been too focused on the SUV careening toward her daughter.

A crowd of people from the Neeps and Tatties parking lot flooded across the street, and customers from Bread on Arrival poured out to add to the chaos. The newcomers swarmed around them, asking what had happened and whether anyone had been injured.

Molly thanked everyone for their concern, then hustled Chloe and Angus toward Bread on Arrival, swinging around the big Victorian to go in the back entrance. "I'm going to call the police," Molly said when they were inside. "You head on up with Angus, okay?"

Chloe nodded. She was clearly shaken, but followed Molly's direction without remark. That alone showed how much the near disaster had upset her daughter. Molly made the call, then quickly updated Laura and Carol.

"That's horrible," Carol said. "And you say the driver didn't stop? Could he have not seen Chloe?"

"I don't see how he could have missed her." Then the double meaning of what she'd said made Molly start shaking. She hadn't seen how the SUV could miss Chloe, and the fact that her daughter was all right was the most unreal part of all. "Can you send the officer up when he or she arrives?" Molly asked. "I want to be with Chloe."

Carol gave her a quick hug. "Of course. You go."

By the time Officer Dalziel Murdoch arrived, Molly had brewed Chloe a cup of tea. Angus had apparently found the entire morning exhausting, as he merely drank some water and flopped down on his dog bed in the corner. Molly and Chloe sat by the window of the kitchenette and spoke to the officer, a blond 27-year-old relatively new to the force.

"I've already spoken to witnesses from Neeps and Tatties," he explained. "When I was told you were all right, I felt it best to secure information from the witnesses who were most likely to leave."

"That sounds smart," Molly said. Though all the officers on the Loch Mallaig police department were competent, she was disappointed that Greer hadn't answered the call. She knew Greer much better. And Officer Murdoch's tendency to twitch nervously didn't help calm her own nerves.

"Although I have a good description of the vehicle," the officer continued, "I have no description of the driver. Can you tell me anything?"

Chloe shook her head. "It happened fast. I was crossing the street to talk to the owner of Barking Plaid, who flagged me down. I met her at the pet store yesterday and gave her some advice about her beagle's anxiety. One moment I was crossing, the next I felt the SUV brush by me."

"Chloe, do you think this could have been Camden?" Molly blurted out. "He did send you flowers out of the blue, and his behavior sounds odd."

"Camden?" Officer Dalziel repeated, blinking rapidly.

"Camden Landry," Chloe said. "But Camden didn't try to run me over. He's not that kind of person. Honestly, Mom, he's a nice guy. We never even had an argument. Plus, Camden drives a little hybrid car, not an SUV."

The officer cleared his throat. "Is he local?"

"He lives in Milwaukee," Chloe said.

Officer Murdoch blinked. "Why do you suspect him?"

"The pile of strange coincidences," Molly said. "Within a day of Chloe arriving for a visit, we've had vandals setting a fire and throwing paint, and now someone nearly runs over Chloe and Angus. What if it's all related somehow?"

"How?" Chloe asked. "I haven't had any arguments with anyone, not even clients at the clinic. No one could possibly want to hit me with a car. It had to be an accident."

"It is improbable that the vandalism and the street incident are related," the officer said. "The driver could have been on his phone or otherwise distracted, and foolish. As for the vandalism, the timing also coincided with The Wandering. We got a number of complaints last night about the event."

"Complaints?" Molly asked.

The officer twitched a shoulder in a shrug. "Mostly noise complaints, some jaywalking, and some littering. But the bakery was a strong proponent of The Wandering. Maybe someone was angry about it. Now that it's over, that should stop."

"I hope so," Molly said. "This has been a bad couple of days."

The officer tipped his head in agreement, then finished his questions and left. Molly walked him to the door that led to the outside stairs. When she returned to the kitchen, Chloe was staring at her phone.

"What's up?" Molly asked.

Chloe cleared her throat nervously, reminding Molly of the officer who'd just left. "I got a text from Camden. He's here in Loch Mallaig and wants me to come and see him. He says he wants to apologize."

"He's here?" Molly stiffened in alarm. Despite Chloe's constant assurances that Camden was a nice guy, Molly didn't appreciate the coincidence of finding out the man was in town right after someone had nearly run over Chloe.

"At the Two Scots Guesthouse. He says we need to talk. He wants to explain. I think I should go."

"Absolutely not," Molly said. "This is one coincidence too many. You need to stay away from that man." Molly realized she'd overplayed the mom voice when Chloe's expression turned mulish, exactly as it had when Molly put her foot down in Chloe's teens.

"I'm going," Chloe said. "I have questions and I want answers."

"Fine," Molly agreed finally. "As long as I come too." At first, she thought Chloe would argue over that, but her daughter acquiesced—albeit with a slight eye roll. *Guess there's still some teenager in there after all.*

———————— ❈ ————————

After telling Laura and Carol the plan, Molly and Chloe drove over to the Two Scots Guesthouse. As they parked in front of the Tudor-style house with classic brown beams on white siding, Molly spotted two SUVs in the lot, both dark colored. "Chloe, could one of those have been the car that nearly hit you?"

Chloe peered at the vehicles. "I'm not sure. I was terrified in the moment. They look too similar for me to venture a guess."

Molly wasn't sure either. Her memory of the SUV that had nearly hit Chloe was that it had been huge, but she couldn't be sure of the accuracy of that impression.

"Mom, if you worry over every SUV in Michigan, you're going to make yourself crazy," Chloe said. "And the officer could be right. The driver was probably on his phone or otherwise distracted, and it was simply a near accident."

"Too near," Molly said.

The small guesthouse served a full breakfast for guests, but an additional light tea was available throughout the day to anyone. It offered an inexpensive lunch spot mostly patronized by Loch Mallaig locals. As most of the pastries for the tea came from Bread on Arrival, Molly knew and liked the proprietors, Ewan and Myra Loganach.

When they entered the small dining room, Molly was surprised to find it empty. Granted, it was midafternoon and she supposed it was a little late for lunch. How had the day passed so quickly? "Didn't you say Camden was meeting you here?"

"He's probably upstairs, running late," Chloe suggested. "We can wait. I don't mind a chance to gather my thoughts."

They'd barely settled at a table when the swinging door to the kitchen burst open and Georgia Pinter hurried over to their table. "Hi," she said enthusiastically. "How nice to see you. Can I get you some tea?"

Molly exchanged glances with Chloe. They'd both had a large mug of tea in the apartment. Molly shook her head. "None for me."

"None for me either," Chloe added.

"The tea is free," Georgia said, dropping her voice conspiratorially. "It's only the pastries and cheeses that cost money."

"Water will be fine," Molly said. Her stomach growled, and she added, "And a cheese plate."

"Okay," Georgia said, her tone suggesting she thought they'd made a poor choice.

Chloe pulled out her phone. "I'm going to text Camden."

"Good idea." Molly's gaze remained on the kitchen door. She found Georgia a little unprofessional and wondered where Myra was since she usually served tea.

"Camden says he's on his way," Chloe told her mother.

Before Camden appeared, Georgia returned with a tray bearing a cheese plate, an assortment of cookies, and a pot of tea. She arranged it all on the table. "I know you said you just wanted water, but this peppermint tea is delicious. And I made the cookies. I'd love to hear what you think of them."

Chloe thanked her for being thoughtful, and Georgia beamed at her. Molly wasn't sure *thoughtful* was the word she would have chosen, but her nerves were a little frayed from constant concern about Chloe. She managed to murmur something positive before Georgia hurried to the kitchen.

"I think she means well," Chloe said as she picked up a piece of cheese and nibbled it.

Molly almost laughed. When Chloe was little, she'd often eaten cheese that way, reminding Molly of a mouse.

Chloe's eyes widened suddenly and she stood up. "Camden."

The man in the doorway focused on her. He was tall, the top of his head only a few inches below the doorframe. He wore a tailored blue suit, and the shirt under it was open at the throat with no tie. His hair was slightly tousled and his face was flushed, making Molly wonder if he had been napping or if he was simply nervous.

"Chloe," he said. "Thank you for coming." His gaze slid toward Molly.

"This is my mom, Molly," Chloe said.

Camden brightened slightly as he walked across the room, his hand out. "Pleased to meet you, Mrs. Ferris." He waved at one of the empty chairs. "May I join you? I have a lot of explaining to do."

"Of course." Chloe sank into her own chair.

Camden sat. Molly pushed one of the cups toward him, and he poured himself some tea. Then he picked up one of the cookies on the plate in the middle of the table and took a tiny bite, reminding Molly suddenly of Chloe, though she suspected Camden was using it as a stalling tactic.

Chloe clearly wasn't interested in stalling. "You wanted to tell me something?"

He sipped his tea, then finally spoke in a rush. "I treated you terribly, and I'm sorry. I trusted the word of people who are apparently quite untrustworthy. And I never gave you a chance. I'm sorry."

"What people?" Chloe sounded confused. "What are you talking about?"

He set the cookie directly on the tablecloth and pulled out a handkerchief to dab at his forehead. "Forgive me. I'm feeling a little unwell."

Chloe's expression grew concerned. "What's wrong?"

He shook his head, then winced. "I'm not sure. I'm feeling flushed. Could we continue this later? I know I owe you an explanation, but I think I should go lie down."

"Should you see a doctor?" Molly suggested.

"No. I'm sure I'll be fine." He stood and reached out to touch Chloe's hand. "I do want to talk."

"And we will," she assured him. "For now, you need to focus on feeling better. Can I help you upstairs?"

"I can't believe what an idiot I've been." He shook his head. "I'll be fine. And I'll text you when I wake up."

He left the room then, and though he moved slowly, he was steady enough on his feet.

"That was odd," Molly said when he was gone.

"It could be food poisoning," Chloe replied. "I wish he'd let us take him to the doctor."

Suddenly, they heard a scream from outside the dining room.

Molly and Chloe leaped to their feet and raced out. In the foyer, at the foot of the steps, Camden lay in a crumpled heap. Georgia stood over him, her hand over her mouth and her eyes wide. Another woman knelt at his side, weeping.

Chloe rushed over, nudging the weeping woman aside as she felt for Camden's pulse. Then she flipped Camden onto his back and began CPR. "We need an ambulance!" she shouted to Molly. "Now!"

6

An ambulance arrived even before the police, and the paramedics instructed Chloe to stop performing CPR. From the behavior of the EMTs, Molly doubted Chloe's efforts had done any good.

Chloe stood beside her mother, holding herself rigidly upright, which Molly suspected was because she was struggling against hysteria. There was enough of that in the room, between Georgia wringing her hands and the unknown woman keening. The ambulance team had to physically move the stranger to do their work—or try to.

When Deputy Police Chief Broderick Gillespie arrived on the scene, Molly found the man's quiet authority made her feel instantly more composed. He surveyed the group and came directly to Molly. "Do you know this man?"

"I didn't until today," Molly said. "Chloe knows him from Milwaukee." She gestured toward Chloe. "This is my daughter, Chloe Ferris."

Chloe tore her gaze away from the ambulance crew to blink owlishly at the deputy chief.

His gaze took in both of them. "I could have guessed. Miss Ferris, can you tell me his name?"

Chloe swallowed hard. "Camden Landry. We went on a few dates in Milwaukee."

"It must have been serious for him to come all the way to Loch Mallaig with you," Gillespie suggested.

Chloe shook her head. "He didn't come with me. We weren't

55

seeing each other anymore. Camden said he'd come to Loch Mallaig to talk to me, to tell me why he broke it off. But then he got sick suddenly and left the dining room to go lie down in his room upstairs." She blinked rapidly and her voice took on a strained edge. "He didn't make it."

"So he was with you shortly before his collapse?" the deputy chief asked.

"With both of us," Molly interjected.

"Because they killed him!"

This shrieked accusation startled everyone. It came from the woman who'd been weeping and moaning at Camden's side. Now she stood where the emergency crew had gently moved her. Her expensive, steel-gray pantsuit was disheveled from her time on the floor, and her hair was equally wild, matching the expression on her face. She jabbed a finger at Chloe. "That little gold digger did something to my brother."

"What are you talking about?" Chloe asked.

"Who are you?" Molly demanded.

The deputy chief hushed them all as he stepped closer to the stranger. "Camden Landry is your brother? Can you give me your name, please?"

"Kaitlin Landry." She said her name in a tone that suggested they all should recognize it.

"Did you come to Loch Mallaig with your brother?" the deputy chief asked.

"No. Camden snuck away from his work at a critical time for the business. He was all worked up about *her*." Kaitlin waved a perfectly manicured hand toward Chloe. "His business partner asked me to follow him and get him home to work. I agreed because I thought the little gold digger might hurt my brother. And now she has!"

"That doesn't make any sense," Molly said.

"You should arrest both of them," Kaitlin snarled. "They're probably in it together."

"We haven't determined what happened to your brother," Gillespie said. "Does he have any serious medical conditions?"

"No." Kaitlin's declaration was ice-cold as she glared at Chloe.

Molly glanced at her daughter and realized Kaitlin's glare was lost on Chloe, whose focus was on the ambulance team.

"I should go clean up," Georgia finally said, as she edged toward the dining room. "The Loganachs will be angry if I leave the food on the table."

The deputy chief stepped in front of her. "Did Camden Landry consume anything in there?"

"Yes," Molly said. "He drank some tea and ate a bite of one of the cookies."

"In that case, don't touch anything on the table," Gillespie commanded Georgia. "I want to examine it."

The paramedics began loading Camden onto a stretcher. Their movements lacked urgency, which Molly read as a bad sign. After they had Camden strapped in, one of the medics walked over to the deputy chief and murmured in his ear. The deputy chief's expression turned stony, then the EMTs wheeled the gurney out of the room.

"I will need to ask all of you to come into the library." He gestured to the doorway on the other side of the foyer. "I have more questions, and we need to move out of this area."

Chloe forced her gaze away from the front door that the gurney had passed through. "Is Camden dead?"

"He hasn't been pronounced," the deputy chief said. "He's on the way to the hospital."

"He didn't have a pulse," Chloe said.

"No."

Tears ran down Chloe's face, but she didn't make a sound. She merely walked into the library as Kaitlin began wailing again. Molly studied the wailing woman and noticed that her eyes were now dry, despite her sounds of distress.

The library at the Two Scots Guesthouse was small and cozy. One wall was lined with floor-to-ceiling bookshelves, and several overstuffed armchairs filled the rest of the space. Molly and Chloe settled into chairs near the room's single window. Molly immediately regretted their choice as a chilly draft came off the old window glass, which was likely original to the 100-year-old Tudor-style house.

Deputy Chief Gillespie waited for each of them to sit, then stood near the fireplace, producing a notepad and pen from a pocket. "I want to hear about the last conversation each of you had with Camden Landry. We'll begin with you, Ms. Landry."

"I checked in late Thursday night, as it took me some time to find out where Camden was staying," Kaitlin said. "He wasn't in his room. I wasn't able to speak to him until yesterday. He refused to see sense and insisted he wouldn't be leaving this place until he talked to her." She glared at Chloe, adding a distinct sneer to the word "her."

"And did you speak to him today?" Gillespie asked.

"No. I am not an early riser."

"You came by the bakery yesterday asking for Chloe," Molly said, certain that her guess was correct.

"I did," the woman said. "I planned to talk some sense into her since I couldn't get my brother to see reason."

Gillespie added some notes to his pad. "Why were you opposed to your brother dating Miss Ferris?"

Kaitlin's eyes narrowed. "Because she's a gold digger."

Molly bit her tongue to keep from yelling at the dreadful woman.

She noticed Chloe appeared unfazed by the accusation and wondered if her daughter could be in shock.

Gillespie raised an eyebrow. "What made you think Miss Ferris was a gold digger?"

"Because that is the kind of woman my brother is attracted to," Kaitlin said. "We've had this problem before, and Camden's business partner assured me that we were having it again."

Gillespie raised his eyebrows. "And who is your brother's business partner?"

"His name is Nathan Glower," Kaitlin answered.

"And is Mr. Glower also in Loch Mallaig?"

"I have no idea. He didn't tell me his plans, but I think it unlikely. The company is in the middle of negotiations to buy another business. Nathan said the proceedings were delicate."

After a few more questions, the deputy chief thanked Kaitlin for her time, adding, "You should stay in Loch Mallaig until we sort out exactly what happened."

The woman puffed up. "I'll tell you what happened. She killed my brother, and I expect you to arrest her!"

Gillespie's expression didn't change, but Molly could see agitation in his body language. "I appreciate that you've been through a terrible shock, Miss Landry," he said evenly. "But the Loch Mallaig Police Department operates based on evidence, not the orders of bereaved relatives."

Kaitlin stood so suddenly she reminded Molly of a jack-in-the-box. "In that case, I'll be going to my room where I can call my lawyer and see what I have to do to get justice for my brother." She swept out of the room dramatically, leaving Molly to wonder if she hoped for applause at her performance.

The deputy chief faced Georgia. "And when was the last time you had a conversation with Camden Landry?"

The woman knotted and unknotted her hands. "I guess we talked a little when I got him some tea and a cheese plate last night. He said he didn't feel like going out for supper, so he had a late tea instead. He was fine then. He didn't talk much, and I left right after because I wanted to join in The Wandering. I'd seen the posters for it."

"So you can't say what Mr. Landry did last night?"

Georgia shook her head. "I do know he didn't come down for breakfast."

"Did anyone see him? Can anyone tell us if he was well this morning?" the deputy chief asked.

"No. Sorry."

"That's enough for now," Gillespie said. "I'll need to talk to the Loganachs too."

"Mrs. Loganach is in her room, resting," Georgia said. "She hasn't been feeling well the past few days. Her husband isn't here, but I expect he'll be back any minute since we're short handed."

The deputy chief frowned, but didn't immediately speak again. Molly could almost see the thoughts churning behind his dark eyes. Clearly there were things he didn't like here, but what? Finally he asked, "Where do you live?"

"Here at the guesthouse for now," Georgia said. "There's a dinky little room off the kitchen the Loganachs said I could use until I find a place, since I'm new here. They're nice people."

"Yes they are," the deputy chief agreed. "You're free to go back to work, but please avoid the dining room."

She opened her mouth as if to protest, but closed it tight and scuttled out of the room quickly enough.

Deputy Chief Gillespie settled into a chair when it was only Molly and Chloe in the room. Molly didn't know Broderick Gillespie particularly well, but she admired his steady, thoughtful way. She knew his wife, Maureen, a bit better, mostly from her visits to the bakery. She was, in many ways, the polar opposite of the deputy chief. Where his dark coloring reflected his Chippewa heritage, his wife was fair and blonde.

"I'm worried," Molly told him. "The cookie and tea that Camden consumed were served to us as well. If Camden ate or drank something that made him sick, it's possible it was intended for one of us."

The deputy chief smiled slightly. "It's a little early to imagine a poisoner lurking in the shadows, Mrs. Ferris. Mr. Landry's attack may have been completely natural. His sister may simply have been unaware of a medical issue her brother had."

Molly appreciated the tactful way he avoided saying *death*. She suspected Chloe was in a lot more distress than she was letting on.

Gillespie directed his attention toward Chloe. "Before today, when was the last time you spoke with Camden Landry?" His voice was gentle, and Molly realized she wasn't the only one who could see through Chloe's attempt to act normal.

"Weeks ago," Chloe said, and instantly her eyes flooded. She seemed not to notice when the tears overflowed onto her cheeks. "We'd stopped dating. I truly don't know why. Today he suggested it was because people had said things about me, but he didn't tell me who or what was said."

Molly spoke up, barely controlling the flash of anger building. "From what Kaitlin Landry said, I suspect the who was Camden's business partner and the what was something the man made up."

"There are some strange things going on," the deputy chief said. "But not many concrete answers yet." He eyed Chloe again. "How long do you intend to be in Loch Mallaig?"

"Through Thanksgiving," Chloe said. She relayed the story of the bat infestation and the closing of the clinic where she worked. "I'm a veterinarian at one of the most successful pet clinics in Milwaukee. I don't need to date any man for his money, and I've never cared much for material things beyond my basic needs anyway."

The deputy chief spoke gently, "I am certain you are not a gold digger, Miss—Dr. Ferris. Until we do nail down what's happening, I'll ask you not to return to Milwaukee. I feel certain we'll sort this out by Thanksgiving. If not, we'll update you on travel restrictions."

Chloe's face expressed clear distress, but she didn't argue.

"Are you staying with your mother at the bakehouse?" Gillespie asked. At Chloe's nod, he added, "Then I can find you both if I have more questions. In the meanwhile, you can leave. Try not to worry."

Like that's going to happen. Molly gently shepherded her daughter outside. As they moved into the parking lot, Molly spotted the two SUVs again. "Wait a minute," Molly said. "I want to ask if the police will check if either of these could be the one in the near hit-and-run."

Chloe stared at her mother, then shook her head as if clearing it. "I had completely forgotten about that. Do you think it matters?"

"I'll feel better if the police consider it," Molly said.

Chloe gazed toward the guesthouse and shuddered. "I don't want to go back in there."

"I don't blame you." Molly hugged her daughter. "You wait in the car. I'll be right back."

Chloe reluctantly agreed and Molly trotted through the front door. She found Deputy Chief Gillespie talking with Ewan Loganach, who still wore his coat since he'd just returned, but the lawman waved her over when he saw her.

"Your focus is on Camden, as it should be," Molly said carefully. "But Chloe was in a near hit-and-run earlier involving a dark SUV. There are two in the parking lot that are the right color. Could you check to see if either of them could have been involved?"

The deputy chief didn't respond immediately. As he was the kind of man who preferred to consider all the possibilities, it didn't surprise Molly that he watched her silently for a moment as if waiting for her to break down and tell him anything she might be holding back, and she resisted the urge to shift defensively as his gaze stayed on her.

Finally, he refocused on Ewan. "Can you tell me who owns the two SUVs in your lot?"

"One of them is mine," Ewan said. His eyes darted to Molly, and his lips twitched nervously. "I promise I wasn't out trying to run anyone over in it. I used my wife's car when I ran my errands since it gets better gas mileage."

"And the second SUV?" Gillespie asked.

"It belongs to one of our guests." Ewan hesitated. "Camden Landry's sister, Kaitlin."

The deputy chief pursed his lips as he mulled over the answer, but Molly could feel her temper rising. Kaitlin clearly came to Loch Mallaig with an agenda that involved keeping Chloe out of Camden's life. Was she so committed to her agenda that she'd try running Chloe down?

The deputy chief put a hand on Molly's arm, making her jump. "I'll look into this."

Molly wished she could listen in on the follow-up, but she knew she should get Chloe to the apartment. "Thank you."

As she spun and left, she decided that she wasn't simply going to wait around for whatever the police decided to do. Molly had the feeling someone was after Chloe, and Molly had better find out and stop them.

It was the only way she could keep her daughter safe.

7

Sunday morning, Chloe remained quiet and unwilling to talk about Camden. Molly hoped she would benefit from the peace of the church service at St. Andrews, as Molly always did. Unfortunately, she quickly realized that much of the buzz of conversation before the service was about the out-of-towner who died at Two Scots Guesthouse.

Molly considered hauling Chloe out of there. It wouldn't make her daughter feel any better to hear the town gossip about Camden. At the same time, she knew that Reverend Findlay had a knack for sharing exactly the scripture Molly needed to hear to soothe her own troubled spirit. So, she gritted her teeth as she heard the whispers and led her daughter to the pew she often shared with Carol and her family.

Carol reached out and squeezed Chloe's arm, getting a weak smile in return. Molly was glad that Chloe had other people who cared right beside her. There may be some whispered conversations everywhere else, but in this spot, they were family.

As always, the music was uplifting, and Molly was glad to hear Chloe's sweet alto beside her during "A Mighty Fortress Is Our God." When Reverend Findlay came up to the podium, he asked them to open their Bibles to 1 Samuel 16:7 and read aloud, "'The Lord does not see as man sees; for man looks at the outward appearance, but the Lord looks at the heart.'" He then talked about how easy it is to jump to conclusions about people based on the scantest evidence. "We judge people by how they dress, where they are from, what accent they have, or what things we've heard whispered about them. It's understandable. It's human. But it is not godly."

As he continued talking about viewing others through the lens of love and grace, Molly saw tears run down Chloe's cheeks. She took her daughter's hand, and Chloe held on tightly as her gaze stayed fixed on the pulpit, taking in the reverend's words.

When the service ended, Chloe immediately whispered that she needed to go to the powder room.

"Are you all right?" Molly asked in alarm.

Chloe smiled, and Molly was glad to see it was stronger than the one she'd given Carol earlier. "I'm okay. I'll catch up with you outside."

As her daughter hurried up the aisle, pausing only when someone spoke to her, Molly suspected Chloe was probably hoping for a quiet place to hide from too much socializing and from the curious faces that turned Chloe's way as she passed.

Caught up in watching Chloe, Molly jumped when a deep voice spoke her name. She realized Fergus was in the row in front of hers, and he was smiling at her.

"You were deep in thought," he said.

"I must have been," Molly said. "I never noticed you were in the row in front of us."

Fergus chuckled. "I wasn't. I came in late. I actually came up here to chat with you. I heard about yesterday. Are you and Chloe okay?"

Molly had another disparaging thought about the efficiency of the Loch Mallaig gossip network, but she assured Fergus that she was fine. "I think Chloe is grieving. She only went out with Camden Landry a few times, but she liked him."

"It's hard to lose a friend," Fergus said sympathetically. "Especially when it happened right in front of her."

Carol had been absorbed in chatting about Sunday plans with

her family, who filled the rest of the pew, but she clearly heard Fergus. "Molly," she said. "You and Chloe should come home with me for Sunday dinner. I always make enough to feed an army. It'll be a little rowdy with Maisie and Gavin, but that could be good for her."

"Normally she'd love that," Molly assured her. "But I'm not sure Chloe is up for such exciting fellowship today."

"I can understand that," Carol agreed, nodding sagely. "I hope you can come to dinner before she goes back to Milwaukee."

"That sounds wonderful," Molly said, then hugged Carol and waved goodbye to her husband, Harvey, their daughter and son-in-law, Jenny and Craig Gilmore, and their seven-year-old twins before they all filed out of the pew.

Fergus put his hands on the pew to lean closer to Molly. "You two could come have lunch with me."

Molly smiled in appreciation. "That's kind of you, but I'm not sure Chloe is ready for a restaurant either, even one as nice as the King's Heid Pub."

Fergus raised an eyebrow. "I was suggesting I'll cook for you at my house."

Fergus's house was a Georgian manor built by his grandfather in 1971, huge yet homey with gorgeous lake views. It was also far from all the gossiping voices around them.

"I think that would be lovely," she said. "Thank you."

They set a time, then Fergus walked out of his row to walk with her to the vestibule of the church. A number of people spoke to Molly as she passed, but not nearly as many as called out to Fergus. It was obvious which one of them was a native son to Loch Mallaig. Molly's family had merely been vacationers, even though they'd made the trip every year to summer in Loch Mallaig.

When they reached the vestibule, Molly scanned the room, but didn't see Chloe. "I think she may be at the car," Molly said to Fergus. "She was overwhelmed. I'll go find her. See you in a bit."

"Great," Fergus said. "And bring Angus along if you'd like. He'll enjoy the outing, and if Neil happens to pass through, he'd love to see Angus too."

"Neil won't be joining us?"

"He might. I texted an invitation, but he was noncommittal. I think he may have a new girlfriend that he hasn't told me about yet." Fergus chuckled. "At twenty-six, Neil is a grown man, but that doesn't stop him from worrying about how I feel about his dating life. If it grows into something serious, I'm sure I'll hear about it."

"And how do you feel about being shut out?"

"It's not my business unless he wants to tell me."

"A good attitude." Molly's shoulders slumped. "I have to constantly remind myself that Chloe is a full-fledged adult with 'doctor' at the beginning of her name, and I shouldn't be mothering her too hard. I guess I've just never gotten past the desire to protect her from everything."

They exchanged a few more words about the challenges of having adult children, then Molly walked outside and scanned the groups standing on the church lawn, checking for Chloe among them.

She hoped Chloe wouldn't mind her accepting the Sunday dinner invitation. She wanted to talk more with Fergus. He was a good friend and had helped her in the past with some thorny problems. She hoped he would have some insights about the tangled events they'd been caught in since Chloe came to visit.

Molly drifted toward the parking lot, where she spotted Chloe near the car, chatting with Carol and Jenny. By the time Molly reached her, Carol and Jenny had been practically dragged away by their husbands and Jenny's children, leaving Chloe alone.

"How are you doing?" Molly asked.

Chloe gave Molly a faintly exasperated expression. "Is that going to be the opening question for every conversation we have?"

"Sorry," Molly said. "But I am concerned."

"I'm sad, Mom," Chloe said. "But I'm okay. Carol said she'd asked us to Sunday dinner but you vetoed. I hope you didn't do that on my account."

Molly raised her eyebrows. "You wanted to go to dinner at Carol and Harvey's house?"

Chloe laughed. "I suppose not. Not that they aren't lovely, but I'm a little tired. No, I meant that you don't have to feel bad about leaving me alone at the apartment. Angus and I could have shared a sandwich and both of us would be perfectly happy."

"I hope that doesn't mean you couldn't be talked into going anywhere," Molly said. "Because I did accept an invitation to have lunch with Fergus. He's cooking. And he invited Angus too."

"Well," Chloe said, stretching out the word. "I am curious to see Fergus's house. You described it on the phone once as being like something from a period TV show."

"It is spectacular," Molly said. "And it's right on the lake."

"Okay," Chloe agreed. "If Angus is game, so am I."

Angus was truly ecstatic about the Sunday excursion, and his tail wagged for the entire drive around the lake. He always loved an outing, but Molly suspected that it was the addition of Chloe that truly made it special for the little dog. The two had a strong bond, and Molly felt certain Angus would mope after Chloe went home to Milwaukee.

When the Georgian manor came into view, Chloe gave a low whistle. The driveway up to the huge, two-story house was fairly simple with limited plantings, likely to avoid obscuring the view. The house sat above Loch Mallaig at the lake's narrowest spot, which meant the view included both the beautiful blue water and the hillside across the lake. The leaves had fallen off the trees, but Molly knew that same hillside had looked like a mountain aflame only a month before. Now the bare trees showed off the few houses nestled among them.

Everywhere the signs of coming winter were plain. Fergus's home was built of pale stone with an abundance of tall windows. Trellises climbed between the windows, though the vines were mostly bare now. The normally lush lawn was slipping into the golden color of dormancy. In the summer, the light-colored house stood in contrast to the vibrant greens of the trees, but now it matched the chilly transformation that heralded the coming winter.

"Wow, Mom, you weren't kidding," Chloe said. "This mansion is amazing. You always describe Fergus as a childhood friend, but you never mentioned that he's some kind of royalty."

Molly laughed. "Fergus is Fergus, no matter how big his house is. But I do have to admit the place is impressive. Though it's almost skimpy when you compare it to Castleglen. The resort's lodge buildings are huge, with lots of timber and stone."

"I can't wait to see it."

By the time Molly pulled up near the house and shut off the engine, Fergus was walking out to meet them. With his tousled hair, gray-speckled beard, and comfortable sweater and jeans he'd changed into after church, he was a rough contrast to the stately house. As she'd told Chloe, Fergus was Fergus, warm and kind and not nearly as fancy as his house. Angus barked with joy at the sight of one of his favorite humans.

Fergus greeted them warmly and crouched to pet Angus. Then he herded them into the house and gave Chloe a tour of the comfortable yet impeccably decorated first floor before leading them to the spacious, beautifully updated kitchen. The kitchen was unusually shaped, being extremely long with all the cabinets and appliances lined up along one wall. This was because the opposite wall was made up of glass to offer amazing views of the lawn and the lake beyond. A table in front of the windows was set for lunch.

"This is extraordinary," Chloe said. "I'd never go to work if I lived here. I'd spend all my time staring out at the lake."

"It is tempting," Fergus agreed. "I've seen just about all the wildlife Michigan has to offer at one time or another."

Molly joined Fergus in finishing up lunch preparations while Chloe stood at the window with Angus at her feet, both staring out at the lake.

As Fergus was carving a small roast, he whispered to Molly, "How are you both?"

"Not much different than we were at church." The corners of Molly's mouth twitched upward as she remembered her conversation with Chloe about that very question.

Soon they were seated at the table, chatting. Angus remained near the window, avidly gazing outside despite the delicious aromas emanating from the serving dishes. Molly had expected Angus to do a little begging, but he was fully absorbed in whatever his sharp eyes could see beyond the yard. Molly had to agree that it was tough not to stare out the window constantly. The view was spectacular.

"I know Molly is thrilled you could be here for Thanksgiving, Chloe," Fergus said. "Are you going to be able to come to Castleglen for dinner?"

"That's the plan." Chloe flicked her gaze to her mom. "I appreciate the invitation. Mom says the resort is spectacular."

"We're proud of it," Fergus said with a smile. "My son, Neil, will be joining us at Thanksgiving dinner, but I wish Blair could be there too." For Chloe's sake, he added, "Blair is my daughter. She works as a physical therapist in Indianapolis for a private company that focuses on sports rehab."

"That must be a fascinating field," Chloe said. "I wish my patients could tell me where it hurts."

"Blair says she sometimes wishes her clients didn't tell her quite so often," Fergus said with a chuckle.

The conversation lagged for a while as they tucked in to the delicious food. After a few minutes, Chloe spoke up. "I'm okay with talking about yesterday. It was plain that it was on everyone's mind at church today."

Molly blew out a relieved breath. "If you're sure, I would appreciate Fergus's input."

"Sure," Chloe agreed.

"I've heard a lot of stories about what happened," Fergus said, "but I'm not sure how many are true. Catch me up."

Molly did, beginning with the burning of the newspapers and the paint vandalism, then describing Chloe's near accident and the horrible experience at the Two Scots Guesthouse. "I'm concerned about all these incidents, but especially because they could be related," she said when she was done.

"You think a vandal escalated to hurting Camden?" Chloe's tone was deeply skeptical, and Molly noticed her daughter hadn't used the word "killing."

"It all leaves me with a lot of questions," Molly said. "And I want answers, especially if someone is trying to do you real harm. I refuse to believe that near hit-and-run was an accident."

"But I'm not sure if it's wise to push into a police investigation," Chloe said. "I don't want to see you get in trouble, Mom."

"I'm not sure about that," Fergus said, eyebrow raised. "The police would be more concerned if Molly didn't get involved. *That* would be strange."

Molly made a face at him. "You make me sound nosy."

He shook his head, his face the picture of innocence. "Not nosy. Concerned . . . and curious."

Molly suspected she was being teased, but she decided not to rise to the bait. "You know Ewan and Myra Loganach, right? My interactions with them have mostly been through work, and they were always lovely, but I can't say that I'm well acquainted with them."

"I know Ewan better than Myra," Fergus said. "I've played golf with him and we talk shop. He's a nice guy, but forgetful. His wife says he's always one daydream away from walking into a wall."

"I haven't heard that one before," Molly said with a chuckle, then sobered. "Ewan drives a dark-colored SUV, and there was another similar one in the guesthouse lot when we were there. Either one could have been the one that nearly hit Chloe. And I don't like the coincidence of such similar vehicles showing up at another crisis."

"There are a lot of SUVs in Michigan, Molly," Fergus said gently.

"Of course, but I'm positive that this is important." Molly sighed. "I'm thinking it might have been Kaitlin Landry's vehicle that almost hit Chloe."

"We can't be certain that was intentional," Chloe insisted. "And there is no reason to think Camden's sister wanted to kill me."

"She was hostile enough at the guesthouse," Molly replied.

"She was in shock," Chloe said. "Mom, I've dealt with many people in crisis when their pets are sick or injured. If we can't save them, the owners lash out. They're hurting and we're a convenient target. Think how much more someone would be hurting to lose a brother. She was out of her wits."

Molly could see the sense of that, but she wasn't sure she wanted to give up her suspicion of Kaitlin.

"We saw two vehicles at the guesthouse that looked like the one that nearly hit me," Chloe said. "What if the driver was Ewan? Maybe he was daydreaming and didn't see Angus and me. Maybe it was an actual accident all along, and we're blowing it way out of proportion."

"Ewan said he hadn't driven the SUV," Molly reminded her.

"And maybe he said that because he almost accidentally ran me over." Chloe threw her hands in the air. "Maybe this is all a creepy series of coincidences, and the police will call and tell us exactly that. I'm really sad about Camden. I liked him a lot. But I don't see any reason to assume he was murdered."

"Molly, all those things you described are unexpected and strange, but that doesn't mean they're connected," Fergus said. "They sound random. You might be linking them because you want random events to make sense."

Molly felt mildly annoyed that Fergus was siding with Chloe over her, especially when she was worried about Chloe's safety. But she also didn't want to argue with two people she cared about, so she shrugged noncommittally. "You might be right, but I'd feel better if we knew what happened to Camden."

The next day, those very words proved to be nearly prophetic when Deputy Chief Gillespie called the bakehouse early to speak to Molly. "I wanted to tell you that the coroner's report has come in," he said. "Camden Landry died from a drug overdose."

Molly gasped. "What?"

"We tested the dregs in the cup he was drinking from, and the tea was laced with the same drug that killed him." Gillespie paused. "I'm going to have to ask you and Chloe to come down to the police station. I have more questions."

"We'll be there within the hour," Molly said, her mind racing. As she hung up the phone, she thought that the police weren't the only ones with questions. She had big ones herself.

Who would have put deadly drugs in their tea? And exactly who were the drugs meant to kill?

8

The drive to the Loch Mallaig police station was tense and mostly silent, with both Molly and Chloe deep in their own thoughts. Molly's stomach knotted with worry. She needed the police to help keep Chloe safe, and that meant convincing them that someone was after her daughter.

Whether she could do that or not was the question. She'd developed some solid relationships with the Loch Mallaig police. She respected them, and she believed it went both ways, but she was going to be asking for a fairly big leap of faith without a lot of evidence.

As they walked into the station, Molly saw Wilma Guthrie perk up like a pointer dog sighting game. Getting past her without answering a wealth of prying questions would be a challenge. Wilma wasn't mean-spirited, but she took curiosity to a whole new level, and everything she heard she'd be sure to repeat.

Fortunately, Deputy Chief Gillespie appeared at that moment and walked around the reception counter to greet Molly. "Thank you for coming in," he said, his voice kind and quiet. He gestured toward a wooden door that would detour them away from reception. "Come this way."

Molly snuck a last glance at Wilma and saw her reach for the phone. Molly felt a wave of gloom knowing Wilma would be connecting to the Loch Mallaig gossip network as quickly as possible.

"I am aware that this is a lot to ask," the deputy chief said as they walked. "But now that we know Camden's death wasn't natural, we need to rethink everything."

"I understand," Chloe said.

Molly agreed as well, wincing as her stomach knotted more tightly. She knew she wouldn't be nearly so stressed if she were the one in peril, but Chloe was both a more believable suspect and a more logical next victim. Molly's motherly instincts raged at her to defend her daughter, but from what?

They stopped in front of another wooden door. Two straight-backed chairs rested against the wall beside the door.

"I will need to ask you both questions, but separately," Gillespie said. "Mrs. Ferris, will you wait here?"

"Of course." Molly gave Chloe's hand a squeeze, then settled in a chair and found it every bit as uncomfortable as it had appeared at first glance. She watched her daughter proceed the deputy chief into the room and noticed with concern how pale Chloe had become.

After the door closed behind the deputy chief and her daughter, Molly pulled out her phone and sent a quick text to Carol saying that she and Chloe were going to be questioned separately and that she couldn't be sure when she'd return to work. Within moments she got a supportive reply that ended with a promise to check on Angus regularly.

"Oh Angus," Molly said softly, feeling guilty that she'd barely given her dog a second thought as she and Chloe had rushed to leave for the police station. She hadn't thought they'd be gone long, and she appreciated Carol's offer to check on him.

Since she already had her phone in her hands, she passed the time by making a list of what she wanted to find out. Her biggest question was who had convinced Camden to stop dating Chloe. Was it Kaitlin or was it Camden's business partner, Nathan Glower? And was Camden's business partner currently in Milwaukee? She assumed he was, which would take him off the hook for the near hit-and-run and for poisoning Camden's tea. But if he was in Loch Mallaig, he'd be a top suspect since Molly believed it was Chloe who had been meant to drink the tea, not Camden.

The more things Molly put on her list, the more convinced she became that the prime suspect for the car incident and the murder was Camden's sister. Kaitlin owned an SUV, and she had strong feelings about Chloe. And she was right there at the guesthouse, so she could have easily doctored the tea.

"Molly?"

Molly glanced up from her phone to find Officer Anderson standing over her.

Greer sat down on the hard chair beside Molly and laid a hand on her arm. "I heard you were coming in today about the death at Two Scots Guesthouse. Are you okay?"

"I haven't been interviewed yet." Molly tilted her head toward the door. "Chloe is in there, and I'm worried about her. This is a lot. She knew the victim, and she cared for him."

"Deputy Chief Gillespie is a good guy," Greer assured her. "He won't bully Chloe."

"No, I don't expect he will, but I can't help being worried."

Greer changed the subject, obviously trying to distract Molly. "Are you ready for the holiday concert?"

"Not exactly." The Piping Yoopers' holiday concert scheduled for after Thanksgiving felt distant, though it was just short of two weeks away. As a beginning piper, Molly would only be performing on one song. She hadn't practiced since Chloe arrived, and it didn't seem important at the moment. "If I can't get the song down, I'm sure you'll all muddle along without me."

"You're too hard on yourself," Greer said, "and I don't only mean about your piping."

Before Molly could respond, the door opened and Chloe came

out. She was even paler than when she'd gone in, and her hands were visibly shaking.

Molly sprang to her feet. "Chloe, are you all right?"

"I'll be fine." Chloe's expression became apologetic. "Do you mind if I go on back to the apartment? I have a blinding headache. I can catch a cab and see you there."

"A cab won't be necessary," Deputy Chief Gillespie said. "Officer Anderson, will you drive Dr. Ferris?"

"Of course," Greer said.

"Thank you," Chloe responded at little more than a whisper.

Molly knew Carol and Laura would watch over her daughter at the bakery, but she hated that she couldn't leave with Chloe. The second Chloe and Greer were out of sight down the hall, she whirled on the deputy chief. "What did you say to her?"

"Nothing cruel, I promise," he said, holding up both hands defensively. "Please, come in. I'm sure you're eager to get this over with and go home to your daughter."

Molly took a deep breath and marched into the room, where a plain table and several more of the same uncomfortable chairs made up the only furniture. She plopped into one.

"Can I get you a cup of coffee?" the deputy chief asked.

"No thank you. Let's get right to the part where you tell me what you did to Chloe."

"I asked her some questions about her relationship with the deceased." Gillespie's tone suggested Molly was pushing the limits of his temper.

"Did you find out if Kaitlin Landry's SUV was the one that nearly ran over Chloe?" Molly asked. "And I'm wondering if Camden's business partner is still in Milwaukee, since apparently he's the one who started the lie about my daughter being a gold digger."

The deputy chief crossed his well-muscled arms across his chest. "I'm not in the habit of answering questions during an interview," he said, though the earlier annoyance was gone from his face, and he appeared almost amused.

"What about the drug that was in the tea? How common is it?"

Gillespie sighed and gave in. "The drug used to poison Camden would be difficult for the average citizen to get hold of, though apparently not hard for a doctor or a veterinarian."

"Chloe would never hurt anyone," Molly insisted. "She wouldn't even let me set mouse traps in the house when she was a kid. Plus, she cared for Camden. The most negative thing she ever felt about him was hurt, and he came all the way to Loch Mallaig to apologize for that."

"Yes, she told me. But Camden's sister said he was afraid of Chloe."

Molly groaned. "I expect that's a lie. He sent flowers, and though we didn't get to talk to him long at the guesthouse, he didn't act afraid." She leaned forward, placing her palms flat on the table. "Or does my opinion count for anything?"

"It counts for a lot, Molly. I only want to find out what happened."

"Well, one thing that happened was poison was found in tea meant for Chloe and me. Camden may not have been the intended victim, which means my daughter is in danger."

"Or a man was poisoned by the tea that you and Chloe both had access to."

Molly ignored the insinuation. "Who else had access to the tea in the kitchen?"

"We're not completely sure, as we've had some conflicting witness statements," Gillespie said. "But we know Georgia Pinter had access, and we're looking into her background. She said she'd met you before, on the night of The Wandering."

"She chatted with Chloe and me at Bread on Arrival," Molly said. "She seems nice."

But she did have access to the tea. And she was living at the guesthouse where Kaitlin was staying. Could she have put something in the tea at Kaitlin's request? Or had Kaitlin been in the kitchen and paid Georgia to lie? Molly made a mental note to talk more with Georgia Pinter.

"I am glad you're looking into Georgia," Molly said. "But I also hope you're not taking anything Kaitlin Landry says at face value."

"I'm investigating everyone and everything," Gillespie assured her.

The deputy chief ran through more questions about Chloe's movements since she'd arrived. Molly made sure to tell him about Kaitlin coming to the bakehouse asking for Chloe, and she suggested he talk with Kaitlin about it.

With neither of them learning much from the other, the deputy chief finally concluded his questions. "You can go home now," he told Molly, "but it would be best for the investigation if you stay out of it."

Molly didn't comment. Inwardly, however, she vowed to do whatever was best for her daughter. The police could worry about their own investigating.

When she got to the bakehouse, Carol greeted her in the hallway outside the kitchen. "I gave Chloe something for her headache when she came back," Carol said. "I just checked on her. She's asleep on the sofa with Angus."

"This hasn't been much of a vacation for her," Molly said woefully. "Usually we have more to be thankful for during Thanksgiving."

"You have plenty. Chloe could have been injured by that SUV driver, but she and Angus are fine."

"And the fire didn't catch the bakery," Laura said, popping her head out of the kitchen door. "And the red paint washed off. Two more things for us to be thankful for."

"And neither you nor Chloe drank any of the tainted tea," Carol added at the end. "That's nearly miraculous."

"Not really," Molly said. "We hadn't ordered the tea because we'd had some at the apartment before we left. Georgia brought it out because she wanted us to try the flavor." She paused. She should have told Broderick Gillespie that Georgia had been eager for them to drink the tea. "I need to call the deputy chief. After that, I want to talk to Ewan Loganach about Georgia. Can you two spare me a little longer?"

"Of course," Carol and Laura agreed together.

"Are you sure you want to poke around in this?" Carol added. "It may have already put you and Chloe in danger."

Molly stood up straighter. "And that's why I'm going to keep poking until I get answers enough to keep Chloe safe."

She spun and walked out through the front end, intending to grab a coffee before she left. She knew she should stop and eat something, but she was eager to talk to Ewan. She could call the deputy chief about the tea once she got to the quiet of her car.

She was pouring coffee when Kaitlin Landry burst through the door. "You and your daughter killed my brother!" she shrieked at Molly. "And you're not going to get away with it!"

9

Molly's initial shock at the bold accusation—made in front of the bakehouse's current customers—froze her for an instant, long enough for Laura and Carol to rush out. They passed Molly, clearly intent on dealing with the angry woman.

"Go on out the back door," Laura told Molly as she hurried by.

Molly would have liked to question Kaitlin, but she doubted it would prove worthwhile, so she followed Laura's direction and left. She knew Carol and Laura would text her if Kaitlin said anything she should hear.

Upon reaching the Two Scots Guesthouse, she noticed immediately that only one SUV sat in the parking lot, reminding Molly again that the ranting woman in the bakery could easily have tried to run over Chloe. Once again, Molly was glad Chloe was safe with Laura and Carol.

When she got to the dining room, Ewan walked out from the kitchen and his face registered surprise. "Did you come for tea, Molly?"

Molly shook her head. "I was hoping to ask you and Myra some questions."

"Sure. Myra is in the kitchen. She ought to be in bed, but she won't listen to me. Maybe you can talk some sense into her."

Molly followed Ewan into the scrupulously clean kitchen. It was considerably smaller than the kitchen at Bread on Arrival, and no effort had been made to update the room since probably the 1940s. There were no walk-in coolers, of course, but the refrigerator was newer than the hulking gas stove, which resembled a prop from a period movie.

The cabinets and fixtures were in perfect condition, as though the room were a museum exhibit, and the overall mint-and-white color scheme added to the vintage vibe.

At a tiny dinette table, Myra Loganach sat with a cup of tea. Her short, brunette hair was slightly mussed, and she was thinner than when Molly had last seen her. Dark circles under her eyes added to her sickly appearance. But the smile she gave Molly was warm and open. "It's nice to see you, Molly," she said. "I'd stand, but Ewan would probably tackle me."

"Don't worry about that." Molly waved the offer away. "I heard you weren't well."

"I'm feeling much better today, and I can't stay in bed forever." She gestured toward the seat across from her, and Molly slipped into it.

Ewan crossed his arms and frowned down at his wife. "You should have stayed in bed today."

She shook her head. "And leave you to handle everything? Fat chance."

He threw his hands in the air. "What's to handle? We're not exactly being rushed with customers since people are saying we serve poisoned tea."

Molly winced. She hadn't considered the possible effect on their business. "Gossip passes."

"I hope so," Ewan said. "At least no one has checked out yet. But I'm not thrilled that Georgia ran off."

Molly's attention sharpened. "Georgia Pinter? She's not here?"

"She quit this morning," Myra said as she lifted her cup of tea for a sip.

"She wouldn't even work the breakfast," Ewan said. "And I'm not sure the guests appreciated my cooking."

Myra chuckled, setting the cup down. "You could have woken

me up. And you can't blame Georgia for not wanting to stay here after seeing a guest dead on the floor." Then she cringed. "Sorry, Molly. I know the man was a friend of yours."

"Not mine, but my daughter knew him," Molly replied. "Can you tell me where Georgia went?"

Myra shook her head. "She didn't leave an address. It was all a bit surprising, actually."

Surprising and suspicious. "What did you think of Georgia?" Molly asked.

"She didn't seem to have much experience," Ewan said. "She was clearly bright and pleasant, but she made a lot of mistakes. I think the guests overlooked her shortcomings, and I was grateful she was here since Myra was ill."

Molly fixed a sympathetic gaze on Myra. "What was wrong?"

"Can't say for sure," Myra replied as she turned her teacup slowly on the table. "I was exhausted and had an upset stomach, but not enough to warrant a trip to the hospital. I didn't get dehydrated. It was all odd. I don't think I was contagious, because Ewan's fine. In fact, he's been playing nurse on top of running the inn. Otherwise I wouldn't dream of being in the kitchen until I was fully recovered."

"And you hired Georgia right after you got sick?" Molly asked.

"Yes, though I'd met her the day before," Myra answered. "I didn't think we needed the additional help. We're not usually booming this time of year. But she left her number, and we called when I woke up ill."

"Did you tell the deputy chief all this?" Molly asked.

"Mostly," Ewan said. "He did ask questions about Georgia. And, of course, he interviewed her as well."

Molly suddenly had a thought. "I'm curious as to how Kaitlin Landry managed to be right on the scene for her brother's death. Do you know if the deputy chief asked her?"

Ewan shrugged. "Couldn't say. I didn't hear his interviews. But she is staying here. She could have been downstairs in the kitchen. She and Georgia had grown quite friendly in a short amount of time. Georgia had that effect on people."

"You allow the guests in the kitchen?" Molly asked.

"We're casual here," Myra said. "We don't keep the kitchen off-limits to guests, and they're welcome to come in for coffee or tea throughout the day. I have to admit that I was surprised when Ewan told me Kaitlin and Georgia were chummy. I only met Kaitlin once, but she didn't strike me as someone who made friends easily."

"Which is all the more reason she hung out with Georgia." Ewan chuckled. "I think Georgia could make friends with a rock."

"Do you know what Kaitlin does for a living?" Molly asked.

Ewan's expression darkened. "We don't normally poke into the lives of our guests. But she said something to her brother about working with him, and he laughed." He rubbed his hands on his jeans, and Molly got the feeling she might be overstaying her welcome. Still, he said, "I think I have the name of the company. Do you want me to look it up?"

"That would be lovely." Molly assumed Chloe knew the name of Camden's company, but she didn't want to bother Chloe with any more of this than she had to.

"No problem." He dashed from the kitchen.

"Ewan isn't good at standing around." Myra grinned wryly. "He has a lot of nervous energy, and he probably used up his well of patience hovering over me all morning."

"I'm sure it's been worrisome, having you sick."

Myra nodded. "I'm normally such a healthy person, but I am exposed to a lot of germs with guests coming and going. I've been lucky before now. At first I almost thought it could have been food poisoning, except all I've eaten is my own cooking, and Ewan was fine."

"Illness is unpredictable, I suppose," Molly said, though she wondered. Myra lifted her cup to sip her tea again, and Molly's gaze swept the kitchen. Near the door that led out to the backyard, she spotted a key rack. "Are the vehicle keys on there?"

"I hope so," Myra said, then responded to Molly's quizzical glance. "Ewan is terrible for leaving the keys all over the place. You wouldn't believe the number of scavenger hunts I've been on for car keys. That's when I put up the rack. It's been better since then."

"Sounds smart," Molly said, but she also noted that the keys were readily available to anyone staying at the guesthouse.

As Myra seemed to be getting tired, Molly left after Ewan returned with the business name, Prognostechnology, scrawled on a piece of paper. She wanted to get to the bakery, though if she were being honest, that was less a reflection of her work ethic than a need to check on her daughter and find out what had happened with Kaitlin.

She parked at the bakehouse and had barely hopped out of the car before a vaguely familiar man in a dark suit stopped her. It took Molly a moment to realize it was the tall stranger from The Wandering.

"Mrs. Ferris?" he asked.

"I'm Molly Ferris," she acknowledged.

He held out a hand. "I'm Nathan Glower, Camden Landry's business partner. I was hoping you'd have a few minutes to speak with me."

Molly stared at him in shock. Since she'd seen him at The Wandering, that meant he'd been in Loch Mallaig when his partner died. She wondered if the police knew that.

"Mrs. Ferris?" the man pressed, breaking through her surprise. "Can we talk?"

"Of course." Molly was eager to question the man, but not as eager to have all the Bread on Arrival customers watch her do it. "How about if we go over to Neeps and Tatties? We can have a quiet conversation there. If we go in the bakery, we'll be interrupted much more."

"Good idea," the man agreed.

Molly felt a twinge of unease as she crossed the street, but watched carefully for any moving vehicles. They made it to the door of Neeps and Tatties without incident. The restaurant wasn't brightly lit, and there were few patrons. They settled at a small table in the corner.

Before they could begin talking, a waitress appeared. "Can I get you two something to drink?" she asked.

Nathan rubbed his face and asked for coffee, while Molly simply asked for water with lemon. As the young woman bustled away, Molly studied the businessman. He was paler than she remembered, though she supposed it could be from the poor lighting in the restaurant. "Are you feeling all right?"

"Tired," he said. "This has all been a shock."

"No doubt." Molly kept her tone carefully sympathetic. "How long were you and Camden in business?"

"Over ten years. He was a friend as well as a partner. I can't believe he won't be at the office when I get there."

"What exactly does your business do?" Molly asked.

"Business software development."

Nathan paused when the waitress appeared with his coffee and Molly's water, then asked if they were ready to order.

"Nothing for me, thanks," Molly said. "I need to get to work."

The waitress smiled. "I'll be seeing you later then. When I get off, I'm coming by to pick up a cake for my mom's birthday."

"Oh, happy birthday to your mom," Molly said warmly. "I'm sure Carol will have a beautiful cake for her."

"I'm certain of that," the young woman said, then turned to Nathan. "Anything for you, sir?"

"I'll stick with the coffee, for now anyway," he said.

"No problem." The young woman spun and hurried away.

Nathan took a sip of his coffee. "Cam was a brilliant software designer. I think his strength was in his unconventional approach to the work. Unfortunately, he tended to apply his rather whimsical thinking to personal relationships too."

Molly felt a surge of anger at the memory of Kaitlin saying this man had called Chloe a gold digger. "If you're talking about my daughter, she had no interest in anything but Camden's friendship."

Nathan held up his hands. "I don't doubt that. But Camden had a history of falling for some rather ill-suited women who would ultimately break his heart. And then his work would suffer as we all tried to put him back together. He would walk away from projects and not show up for meetings when he was in the middle of one of these situations."

"None of which has anything to do with Camden's friendship with my daughter," Molly said. "Nor does it explain what you said to Camden, what lies you told, to make him upset with Chloe. He moved his dog from the veterinary practice where she works because of what you said."

Nathan groaned, then dropped his gaze to the table. "That wasn't fair." He looked up. "I'm sorry, but we were in the middle of some delicate work, and I did what I thought was best to stop the cycle before it ran its usual course."

"By lying."

"For Cam's own good."

"Really?" Molly asked. "For his own good? Or for yours? If you were concerned about Camden, you would have taken the time to find out my daughter is a fine person and that her friendship with Camden was probably a good thing."

"It's easy to judge me now," Nathan said, his face darkening. "But you're not the one who spent half your life cleaning up after the emotional train wreck that was Camden Landry."

"You sound angry about it," Molly said. "How angry were you when you found out your plan had backfired and Camden was coming here to patch things up with Chloe?"

"I wasn't angry. I was concerned," Nathan insisted. "No matter how eccentric Cam could be, he was the spark behind our company and one of my best friends. I don't appreciate your insinuation, Mrs. Ferris."

"Terrific," Molly said. "Since I didn't appreciate your lies about my daughter. We can both be angry." She rose from the table. "Since I only had water, I'll leave the check to you. Don't forget to tip."

She wove through the tables and out into the sunlight. She knew she'd been anything but a coolheaded investigator in there, but she was a mother above all things, and when she thought of the casual character assassination Nathan Glower had done to Chloe, she wanted to go inside and toss her lemon water at him.

Instead she straightened her jacket and headed toward the street, her eyes darting around, watching for traffic. As she stood at the edge of the Tattie Bogle Road, she thought about how carefully Nathan had painted Camden as his dear friend and as essential to the business. But it sounded as if Camden was a liability as well, and Nathan wouldn't be the first businessperson to consider eliminating a liability.

Molly found herself almost frozen at the edge of the road as she watched an approaching car. She'd simply wait for it to pass. There was no reason to let the sight of a car scare her. She took a deep breath, preparing to step out after the car went by.

Then a hand clamped down on her shoulder. Molly shrieked.

10

"Mrs. Ferris, I'm so sorry," Nathan said, edging away from her. "I didn't realize you hadn't heard me approach. I also want to apologize for being a jerk about your daughter. I'm deeply sorry."

Molly's heart pounded in her chest from the surprise, but she managed to say, "You don't know Chloe." She studied the man's face. He seemed genuinely concerned about how she felt. She might be able to use that to her advantage. "Tell me, Mr. Glower. Who do you think killed Camden?"

He gazed toward the bakery, his face blank, clearly considering the question. He answered without looking at her. "It's tough to say. Cam was so genial. Even when he blew off meetings or missed work, it was hard to stay mad at him." Nathan's pale eyes focused on her. "I don't want to start nasty rumors, but the only person I can think of with motive would be Kaitlin. She's his only family. I imagine she's his beneficiary."

"Is there much to inherit?" Molly asked.

"More than you'd think. Our company has done well, and Cam got the lion's share of the profits." His expression grew rueful. "He was genial, but Cam could negotiate. He knew how important his creativity was to the company."

"Were you staying at the Two Scots with Camden?" Molly asked.

Nathan barked a laugh. "Hardly. Cam never understood the point of spending a lot when he traveled, but I do not share his sentiments. I'm staying at the Moose Lake Country Club. Apparently I barely squeaked in. They're on limited hours for the winter, which explains the service, I suppose."

Molly raised her eyebrows. "I've heard nothing but wonderful things about the Moose Lake Country Club and the service there."

"It's nice overall," he agreed. "But the coffee on my room service tray for lunch was vile. I barely choked down a swallow."

"You should probably mention that to the staff." Molly knew that she'd want to be told if something they'd made at the bakehouse had come out unpalatable without their realizing it.

"I'll tell the front desk when I get back. Right now, I'm going to talk to the police." Nathan reached into his pocket and pulled out a business card, offering it to Molly. "Please call me if there is anything I can do."

"All right." Molly took the card.

"I heard some gossip at the country club that you're something of an amateur sleuth. If you can find out who killed Cam, I'll help any way I can. He made me nuts sometimes, but I loved him like a brother, and I'll miss him."

Molly peered into the younger man's face. He was either a supremely talented actor, or he meant what he'd said about missing Camden. "I'm sorry for your loss," she told him.

She slipped the card into the pocket of her coat, then left the businessman standing in the parking lot of Neeps and Tatties as she returned to Bread on Arrival. Laura and Carol practically swarmed her when she got to the kitchen, eager to hear what Molly had learned while she was out.

"You two first," Molly said. "Anything to tell me about Camden Landry's sister?"

"She's a kook," Carol said with a huff. "She ranted about you and Chloe. Some of the customers got involved in your defense. Laura and I tried to calm the storm, but she wasn't having any of it."

"Did Chloe hear it?"

"We don't think so," Laura said. "Hamish dealt with Kaitlin Landry when he came in for his shift right after you left. He can be wonderfully intimidating when he wants to."

"I'll have to thank him," Molly said. "Have you seen Chloe?"

"She came down a few times for snacks and socializing," Carol said.

"And she looks better," Laura added. "More rested. Now spill. What did you learn?"

Molly ran through her visit with Ewan and Myra, then her unexpected meeting with Nathan Glower. "He doesn't act guilty," she said, "but he was in Loch Mallaig when Camden was murdered. Kaitlin and Georgia were as well, for that matter. I find Georgia's sudden quitting suspicious."

"It could be," Carol said, "but the death of a guest had to be upsetting."

"That's what Myra thought." But Molly wasn't willing to mark Georgia off her suspect list yet. Molly's gaze drifted to the doorway leading to the hall and the stairs. "I'm going to run upstairs and check on Chloe, and then I promise to come and do actual work."

"Good," Laura said. "Because our pecan pie orders alone are staggering. When you come down, I need you chopping nuts."

"Aye, aye," Molly sang out before she ran upstairs. To her surprise, Chloe wasn't there. Instead a note on the refrigerator said, *I've taken Angus for a romp at the park. We'll be back when we start to shiver.*

Molly added her own note to the bottom. *Hope you had fun! Pop downstairs when you get home.*

Once in the bakery kitchen, Molly settled into the task of chopping pecans and blissfully let the room's warmth and cheer soothe her stressed nerves. Chloe eventually returned and joined Molly at the counter. By then, Molly had progressed from chopping pecans for the pies to chopping walnuts for pumpkin bread. As they worked side by side, Chloe talked brightly about her time in the park, and Molly suspected she was intentionally avoiding any more difficult topics.

Because of the long list of orders, the bakehouse kitchen continued to bustle after closing. Molly and Chloe switched to packing up loaves of pumpkin bread for mail orders. It shipped well, so it was one of their most popular mail-order items this season.

Eventually, Chloe excused herself to go play with Angus, and Molly helped Laura and Carol finish up the long to-do list.

"Okay, that's the end of it," Laura finally announced. "Until we start it all again in the morning."

"I could have done without that last part," Carol told her as she took off her apron. "I need to get home and make sure Harvey fed the chickens. He's been working on an article, and he can be as forgetful as a goldfish when he's in the middle of writing." A retired investigative journalist, Harvey still took on freelance jobs from time to time.

Molly closed and locked the door behind Laura and Carol, then scanned the darkened bakery with some relief at the quiet. It had been a stressful few days, and she was ready to spend some time chatting with her daughter.

She found Chloe curled up on the sofa in the apartment, flipping through old photograph albums. Molly sat down beside her, and they shared the memories the pictures provoked.

"I cannot believe I ever wore my hair that way," Chloe said, poking at a family photo. Chloe was beaming a gap-toothed grin, and her hair was cut very short.

Molly gave her daughter a wry grin. "That haircut was precipitated by your attempt to learn hairdressing by cutting your own hair."

Chloe laughed. "Oh, right, I remember that now. You took me to the salon, which I thought was cool, but they nearly had to shave my head."

"You were thorough with the scissors," Molly said, shaking her head. "I almost cried until your dad reminded me that hair grows." She ran a finger lightly over Kevin's smiling face in the photo. "Your dad was a smart guy."

"I know," Chloe said. "And as I remember, he called me Private Chloe for a month while that buzz cut grew out." Chloe laughed. "It's a good thing it happened in the summer. By the time school started, at least I had that much hair." She tapped a photo on the next page. "I came up with a lot of wild stories for why I'd decided to cut my hair."

"You always were creative," Molly said. "You got that from your dad too. He loved to tell a good story."

"I miss him," Chloe said.

Molly wrapped her arm around Chloe's shoulders and squeezed. "Me too. But missing him means we'll always carry him in our hearts, and I can't think of anyone more deserving of that spot."

With one more squeeze, Molly hopped up and headed for the kitchen to fix some dinner. Chloe insisted on helping, and they made a tasty meal of pasta and salad. After they'd finished eating and cleaned up, Chloe offered to take Angus for a walk.

"Let's do it together," Molly said as she snagged the leash from the hook, which instantly resulted in Angus dancing around their feet. "I'm concerned that Angus is going to forget he's my dog with you spoiling him."

"Not spoiling," Chloe insisted. She knelt to pat the little dog while her mother shrugged into her coat. "Appreciating. I wish I could have a dog in my apartment. That's at the top of my list of things to do when I've built up my savings—getting a place where I can have all the animals I want."

"I'm picturing quite a zoo." Molly handed Chloe's coat to her, then snapped the leash on Angus. They headed down the outside stairs and slipped out of the fenced-in yard by the gate.

The night was quiet and beautiful despite the biting chill. The clear sky showed them a sliver of moon like a quirky smile in the sky. They strolled down Loch Mallaig's quiet sidewalks. Darkness fell early in November and brought cold winds with it most nights. The number of people walking on the streets fell sharply this time of year, even with the holidays right around the corner.

After Thanksgiving, Christmas shopping and the season's outdoor events would pull people out, but for now, she enjoyed feeling as if they had the night to themselves. They glanced in windows at each shop, counting how many had given in to Christmas decorating even though Thanksgiving hadn't passed.

"You sound like Gram," Chloe said. "Last time I talked to her on the phone, she was ranting about Christmas decorating before Thanksgiving. She said you'd think Midwesterners would know better."

Molly chuckled. "I can't wait to call her on Thanksgiving. I'll get to hear the Black Friday rant."

"Why would any sane person go shopping in that craziness?" Chloe's imitation of her grandmother's voice was perfect. Then she sighed. "I've been working hard this year, I haven't gotten to see anyone."

"Trying to do everything is one of the great challenges of adulthood," Molly noted.

They'd nearly reached the end of Tattie Bogle Road when a police cruiser pulled up beside them. Molly tilted her head in curiosity as the door swung open and Greer Anderson climbed out of the car.

"Hi Greer," Molly said. "Are you looking for me?"

"It's a nice evening," Greer said, and Molly got the feeling she was stalling. Did Greer have something to say that Molly wouldn't like to hear?

"Any weather you don't have to shovel is nice," Chloe said.

"I hear that," the officer said. "I'm really glad you're able to spend Thanksgiving with your mom. She is very proud of you."

"Very true," Molly agreed.

Greer knelt to pat Angus, and Molly suddenly got the feeling the officer had something to say to them, something she was putting off. Molly almost groaned. Surely the police didn't need to speak to them about Camden again.

"I saw you both out here," Greer said. "And I wanted to give you a heads-up. You'll find out in the morning anyway."

"Find out what?" Molly asked, her stomach suddenly clenching nervously.

"You didn't hear this from me," Greer said.

"What?" Molly and Chloe asked together.

"Nathan Glower is in the hospital." The officer's usually bright eyes were somber. "He collapsed at the country club."

11

"Oh no!" Molly exclaimed, an icy wave of shock crashing over her. "That's terrible. Is he going to be okay?"

"It's too soon to say," Greer told her. "The hospital said he'd been drugged. Gillespie learned you were one of the last people he talked to before his collapse. The waitress at Neeps and Tatties said the conversation was hostile and intense."

"It didn't end that way," Molly said. "He actually apologized for having talked Camden into breaking up with Chloe."

"He did that?" Chloe said, sounding shocked. "I've met Nathan Glower. He has a cat that he brings to the clinic. I thought he was nice."

Greer touched Molly's arm. "Molly, the deputy chief is going to want to talk to you again. The last I heard, he'll be asking for you in the morning. I thought you ought to be forewarned. For what it's worth, I'm convinced you didn't do anything to anyone."

"Thanks, Greer."

Molly and her daughter stood side by side, shoulders touching as the officer walked back to her car and got in. As the car drove away, they stood in the icy cold, facing the darkness that filled in the spot where the police car had been.

Molly went to the police station first thing Tuesday morning, not waiting for a police officer to show up at the bakehouse. Though normally Molly would have thought it impossible to make Deputy Chief Gillespie look that beaten, his angular face was almost haggard. Clearly he was feeling stress. He greeted her warmly enough, but Molly couldn't help but feel nervous. She'd basically been in the thick of all the events of the past days, and she had no explanation for any of it.

"Can I get you coffee or tea?" the deputy chief asked.

"No thank you. I know it's probably silly, but I'm feeling an increasing unease about drinking coffee and tea away from home lately."

Gillespie ran a hand across his short, dark hair. "I think everyone at the station is feeling the same." He led her to the same room where they'd talked before. Molly was disquieted by the familiarity of it all.

"It's good of you to come in," Gillespie said after they sat down. "Though I would have simply called. I don't believe you had anything to do with Nathan Glower's collapse, but I want to hear what you talked about."

"He apologized for being the person who convinced Camden to stop seeing Chloe," Molly said. "And for being the source of Chloe's characterization as a gold digger. He said he was concerned about his business. Apparently Camden had a history of unfortunate relationships that would eventually end badly and affect his work."

The deputy chief raised his eyebrows. "And did you accept his apology?"

"I wasn't happy with him," Molly confessed, "but there is nothing to be done in retrospect. Are you aware that he was in Loch Mallaig when Camden died? As were Camden's sister and Georgia Pinter?"

"How is Georgia Pinter relevant?"

"Apparently she was friendly with Kaitlin Landry, and she quit right after Camden's death," Molly said. "She had access to the tea. Tea meant for Chloe and me."

"I wasn't aware she'd quit. We haven't had her in for more questioning." He leaned back in his chair. "This case has been strange."

"What caused Nathan Glower's collapse?" Molly asked. "Was it the same drug that killed Camden?"

He shook his head. "No. It was dangerous, though. Fortunately for him, he didn't consume nearly enough to be fatal."

Molly straightened, sparked by a memory. "He told me that he'd gotten coffee at the country club, but only drank a little because it tasted bad. Maybe that's when he was dosed."

"We couldn't test the coffee he drank at Neeps and Tatties because the cup had been washed by the time we began our investigation," Gillespie said. "I'm afraid it'll be the same story with the country club."

"You said he didn't drink enough for the dose to be fatal," Molly said. "Does that mean he's going to be all right?"

"Yes, I had a report from the hospital. He's doing much better and will probably be released by the afternoon. I'm going over there after I finish here, and I'll ask him about the coffee he drank at Moose Lake."

After Molly left the police station, she sat in her car and thought about the conversation she'd had with the deputy chief. Nathan Glower's poisoning was almost certainly related to Camden's death. Did that mean Camden had been the intended victim of the tea made for Molly and Chloe? How could the poisoner be certain Camden would drink the tea? It simply didn't make sense. Molly's head spun from thinking about it.

"I need to talk to Nathan," she muttered under her breath before driving to Bread on Arrival. She found the bakery bustling, just as she'd expect with Thanksgiving only a couple days away. Laura and Carol had come in early, and the whole building smelled of cinnamon, cloves, and fresh pumpkin pie.

When Molly entered the kitchen, she was surprised to find Chloe with her sleeves rolled up and a smile on her face. She was lining pumpkin muffins on a tray destined for the display case.

"I'm strictly post-baking chores," Chloe explained at Molly's clear surprise. "I know my limitations."

"Nonsense. Chloe has been a huge help," Carol said, bumping shoulders with the younger woman as she passed. "And we have Bridget packing overnight deliveries for the mail."

"Which means you might want to avoid the front," Laura told Molly. "Hamish is grumbling about being left alone to deal with the mix of customers and gossips trying to learn something new. Speaking of which, how did your police visit go?"

"Deputy Chief Gillespie says he doesn't believe I poisoned Nathan Glower, which is nice," Molly said.

"Of course you didn't poison anyone," Chloe said staunchly.

Molly patted her daughter's arm. "Nathan is going to be okay. He's expected to leave the hospital this afternoon. I know everything is crazy busy here, but I thought I'd bring a box of scones to the hospital for him. I plan to ask him some questions."

"Um, the man was poisoned," Carol said. "Do you think he's going to welcome a food gift?"

"Oh, I hadn't thought of that. Maybe he'll settle for just some conversation," Molly said. "If you think you can spare me."

Laura swiped her hand across her cheek, leaving a flour streak. "Since he's not expected to be released until the afternoon, can you hold off until the morning rush thins out? Hamish could use the help."

As if her mention of his name had called him from the front of the bakery, Hamish appeared in the doorway. "If you hens are done with your *havering*, do you think I could get a hand out front?"

"I'm coming," Molly sang out, getting a curt nod from Hamish.

Molly didn't let the grumpy curmudgeon act bother her. She knew Hamish was as softhearted as they come.

As she began waiting on the line of customers, she quickly learned to recognize the gleam in the eye of those who'd mostly come to gossip. "Do ye think you'll be arrested today?" one sweet-faced elderly woman asked her in a loud whisper. Molly managed to stammer a negative reply.

"I'll have coffee," a craggy-faced man told her, "but Hamish has to make it. I'll nae take a sip of anything poured by you, lass."

That remark earned him a fierce scolding from Hamish.

By the time the morning rush was over, Molly felt as if she'd been through the wringer. She was glad to be leaving, even if it was to go to the hospital.

A short drive brought her to the Kinnaird Medical Center, commonly referred to as the hospital despite offering fewer services than a facility in a larger town. When she reached Nathan Glower's room, she found him dressed and buttoning the top few buttons on his shirt.

"Molly," he said, grinning. "You nearly missed me. I was about to call a cab."

"I would be happy to give you a ride," Molly said. "The bakehouse can spare me an extra few minutes."

"I imagine Thanksgiving must be one of your busiest times," Nathan said, his attention sharpening. "Does the bakery make a good profit?"

Molly blinked at such a forward question. "We're doing well, especially considering we're a fairly new business."

"I heard your head baker has a great background," he said. "I've been to 29 North. Head chef there is an impressive thing to have on her résumé."

"You seem well informed," Molly said.

Nathan laughed, though he did redden slightly. "Sorry. Research is in my blood. As a businessman, I need to know who I'll be dealing with."

"If you'd applied that to Chloe, you would never have called her a gold digger," Molly said.

"All the more reason not to curb my urge to research." He raised an eyebrow. "Want to take back your offer to drive me?"

"No, of course not," Molly said. "I'd like to ask you about the bad-tasting coffee you had yesterday. You said it was on a room service tray, right? Did you see who delivered it?"

He shook his head. "I was on my way to the shower when they knocked. I told them to leave the tray outside. I collected it when I was done in the shower."

"So someone could have tampered with it while it sat outside your door," Molly mused.

"That's what the police said," Nathan confirmed. "Sure, someone could have put something in my coffee, but why? I'm not that bad of a tipper."

Since the last person who'd had something in his drink died, Molly wasn't sure Nathan's attempt at levity was appropriate, but she supposed he was trying to use humor to deal with his own fears. He had to be worried. Someone had tried to poison him.

When she didn't respond to his joke, his face grew serious. "I can't come up with a single reason why someone would try to hurt me," he said. "All businessmen are assumed to have enemies, but I can't think of a soul who'd want to see me harmed."

Just then, a discharge nurse walked in with a pile of papers for Nathan to sign, and Molly appreciated the distraction. She didn't know what to think about the attempt on Nathan's life. He'd apologized, but she couldn't quite let go of the unkindness he'd done to her daughter.

Hospital protocol required that Nathan ride to the exit in a wheelchair. He clearly found the fuss embarrassing, but there was no use arguing with procedure. After balking a little, he gave in and sank into the chair for the ride. A few minutes later, Nathan was settled in the passenger seat of Molly's car.

"How long are you staying in Loch Mallaig?" Molly asked as she navigated out of the parking lot and set out for the short drive to the Moose Lake Country Club.

"I have no idea," he said, huffing in frustration. "The police say I need to stay since I'm part of the investigation, but I have a business to run. And a lot of pressing matters to handle related to Cam's death."

"You told me before that Camden was essential to the business," Molly said. "What happens with that?"

"I'll have to find someone to replace him." He groaned. "As if I could possibly replace Cam. I don't know how we're going to survive."

Not sure how to respond, Molly was slightly relieved when Nathan pulled out his phone and started answering e-mails for the remainder of the drive.

When she pulled up in front of the country club, Molly was struck again by the unique look of the place. The Moose Lake Country Club was a sprawling building with multiple additions put on the original footprint over the years. It had tall peaked rooflines, a few walls sporting dark and white vertical stripes, and dark wood window trims with a distinctly European feel. It wasn't an ugly building, but it did appear as if it hadn't completely decided what style it wanted to be.

"Here we are," Molly said as she pulled under the portico at the entrance.

"Thanks for the ride." Barely glancing up from his phone, Nathan collected his bag of personal effects. "I think I'll head up for a nap. I'm feeling better, but I'm still a little worn out."

"Take care of yourself," Molly said. "And feel free to call if you need something." She fished one of the Bread on Arrival cards from her purse and handed it to him.

"Thanks. You're a nice lady, Molly Ferris." Nathan got out of the car. His stride toward the door didn't waver, but she figured he was probably used to projecting strength. She suspected he was someone who wouldn't want to appear weak.

Her musing had kept her focused on Nathan longer than she normally would have, but it meant she was watching when Nathan opened the country club's entry door—only to be accosted by another man.

The second man was shorter and stouter than Nathan. He wore jeans and a dress shirt with the sleeves rolled up. He waved his hands around as he spoke with evident emotion. Molly leaned toward the window. Why was the man so familiar? She was certain it wasn't someone she knew.

Nathan clamped a hand on the other man's shoulder and the hand-waving stopped, but the man's body language radiated anger. For someone who didn't have any enemies, Nathan had certainly upset this guy. Was this one more person mixed up in the confusion? Molly decided she needed to find out.

She parked in the nearby lot and walked into the country club's lobby. She surveyed the large room, but Nathan and the other man had vanished in the time it took her to park and walk in. Her initial idea of confronting the men had to be shelved.

She nearly left, but then she spotted a familiar face. Actually, it was a familiar hairstyle: a wildly frizzy mop of brassy red curls, presently partially obscured by a simple white scarf. The thin woman in the pale-blue housekeeping uniform stood discreetly off at the entrance to a side corridor. Molly knew the rather high-strung woman from church and the bakehouse, and it took only a moment to come up with her name—Peggy Webster. Molly headed toward her.

The woman's expression reflected her surprise at being approached, but her tone was cheerful. "Hi, Molly. I'm surprised you get any breaks from the bakery at this time of year."

"Hi, Peggy. Sometimes I have to take a break for my own sanity." Molly visually swept the lobby, now conspicuously empty. "It's awfully quiet in here. The last time I was here, I couldn't hear myself think."

"That's the way it goes this time of year, and we're all glad of it," Peggy said. "Just like you, we can use the break. I think early fall is even busier than summer, so we all appreciate the slower pace." Then the woman's gaze darted around. "I really shouldn't stand around and chat. If my supervisor saw me, I'd get quite a scolding."

"I don't want to get you in trouble," Molly assured her. "But I was wondering whether you saw the two men arguing in here a few minutes ago."

Peggy laughed. "Did I? It's the most excitement we've had all week. I didn't think it was fair to be picking on Mr. Glower with him barely out of the hospital." Then she covered her mouth. "I'm not supposed to talk about Mr. Glower's ailment."

Molly raised a hand. "I understand. I'm interested in the man who talked with Mr. Glower. Who is he?"

"He's a guest." Peggy peered around the lobby again, but then her lips twitched in a nervous smile. "It was odd seeing him angry. He's usually pleasant, but he's messy. His room takes twice as long to clean as Mr. Glower's."

"What is the man's name?" Molly asked. "Is his room near Nathan's room?"

"He's a guest," Peggy repeated, her expression worried. "I could get fired for talking about him."

"Of course. I'm sorry. I only wondered because of Mr. Glower's condition. If the man is angry at Mr. Glower and has a room nearby, he could be the one who did something to make Mr. Glower sick. He was clearly angry."

Peggy didn't immediately answer, and the worry on her face grew, but she finally whispered an answer. "It's Mr. Loftis. I'm not sure of his first name. But he isn't always angry. He's usually friendly and nice." She shuffled her feet. "I do have to go, Molly. Don't tell anyone I talked about guests, okay?"

"I won't. I promise," Molly said. "Thanks."

Molly hurried out of the lobby, feeling mildly guilty for upsetting Peggy. As she walked out to the car, she shivered in the cool breeze that was picking up. She glanced up at the darkening sky and suspected rain was coming. If it would hold off until she was back at the bakehouse, she'd be grateful.

On the drive to Bread on Arrival, Molly tried to make sense of Camden's death and Nathan's poisoning. It was ridiculous to think they weren't connected, and despite no one taking her theory seriously, she believed Chloe's near hit-and-run was tied in as well. She was willing to concede the likelihood that the vandalism at the bakery was a prank, possibly by the anti-Wandering contingent, but Chloe's near accident was simply too much coincidence for Molly.

"So who would want to hurt Chloe, Camden, and Nathan?" Molly asked aloud. The person who sprang readily to mind was the volatile Kaitlin Landry. She was staying at the guesthouse with Camden, where she had free access to the kitchen, and therefore to the tea. Plus, her friend Georgia had quit right after the murder. Could that be because she knew who had poisoned Camden and wanted to get away before Kaitlin decided to start tying up loose ends?

Molly had believed Kaitlin a serious suspect when she was only considering Camden's death and Chloe's near accident. Trying to protect her inheritance and get Chloe out of the picture would be great motives, especially if Camden wasn't the intended target for the poison. And she could have wanted to off Nathan if he would interfere with her getting her hands on Camden's money.

But now there was this new person arguing with Nathan, someone named Loftis. Why was the man so familiar? Where might she have met him? It wasn't as if she'd gone many places since Chloe came home and all the craziness began. Had he come into the bakery? She tried to picture the man standing in line at the counter or seated in one of the rustic chairs.

Then it hit her, and she yelped with the memory. Loftis had participated in The Wandering. In fact, he had come up to Molly's table right after Nathan Glower. She hadn't immediately recognized him because Loftis had been pleasant at The Wandering and his face had been twisted with anger when he confronted Nathan at the country club.

Loftis and Nathan hadn't been obviously together at The Wandering, but she did remember seeing them exchange brief conversation at the beverage table. At any rate, it meant that Loftis had been in Loch Mallaig before Camden died. And that put him firmly on Molly's suspect list.

By the time she was walking through Bread on Arrival's back door, she'd run her suspect list through her head a few times, twisting and turning the scant clues she had until she was thoroughly confused. She needed to talk through some of these theories with cooler heads than her own, and she knew exactly where to find them.

In the bakery kitchen, Carol was filling pie shells with pumpkin while Laura mixed dough for dinner rolls. They both were visibly harried, and Molly immediately discarded her idea of asking them for advice about her theories. That decision didn't last long, however, as Laura and Carol both demanded to hear about her outing.

"I'll be glad to tell you," Molly said. "But two things. Where's Chloe? And what can I do to help while I talk? I've skipped out on too much work as it is."

"Chloe is helping out front with Bridget," Carol said. "Hamish had to make a couple deliveries, so we moved Bridget to front duty. Chloe volunteered to help out."

Molly was glad Chloe felt up to facing customers, but she remembered her own time dealing with the more gossip-connected customers, and wondered if Chloe was okay. Her gaze drifted toward the door.

"You can whip up some melting moments," Laura said, interrupting Molly's mother-hen thoughts. "Since we served them at The Wandering, orders for them have been pouring in. They're almost outnumbering the shortbread orders."

Molly swallowed hard. "Melting moments?" She'd made the cookies before, but she had trouble feeling confident with baking for customers.

Carol gave her an encouraging nudge. "It's an easy recipe, Molly. You won't have any problems."

"Fine," Molly agreed finally. "Just let me peek at Chloe first."

"I understand completely," Carol agreed. "If it were Jenny in the middle of all this, I'd be out there like a shot."

Molly gave Carol a grateful smile, then went to the café area. She found Chloe and Bridget with their heads together at the coffee station, giggling like teenagers. Though college-age Bridget was several years younger than Chloe, they'd clearly hit it off. Molly was relieved to see Chloe happy, so she retreated back into the kitchen without interrupting.

She hauled out a mixing bowl and began grabbing ingredients for the cookies.

"Okay, time to spill," Carol said. "How is Nathan Glower?"

"Fine, I think," Molly said. "He told me he didn't see who delivered the coffee that the police believe was the source of the poisoning. He'd told room service to leave it outside the door. Anyone could have accessed it."

"Not helpful," Laura said as she set her dough in the proofer to rise.

"No, but I did see something interesting when I drove Nathan to the country club." Molly went on to describe the argument she'd seen in the entrance. "I went in, but the men had left. I did chat with Peggy Webster. She told me the man's last name is Loftis."

"Interesting," Carol said. "Peggy didn't overhear what they were fighting about?"

Molly shook her head. "I couldn't press her too much. She seemed fairly stressed by talking about guests as much as she did. But as I was driving home, I realized why the angry man, Loftis, was familiar."

"Someone we know?" Laura asked.

"He came to The Wandering at the same time as Glower. That means he was another stranger in town when Camden Landry died."

"Sounds as if we need to learn more about this Loftis guy," Laura said. "I wonder how we could find out his full name."

Carol wiped her hands on one of the cotton cloths they used regularly in the kitchen. "I can think of someone who can help with that."

"Who?" Laura and Molly asked together.

Carol laughed. "Harvey. He fishes with the manager at Moose Lake Country Club, and Harvey can talk a stone into giving up its secrets. Give me a minute, and I'll put him on the case." She slipped her phone out of her pocket and stepped out into the hall to chat with her husband.

Molly tried to concentrate on the cookies, not wanting her divided attention to cause a baking failure. With all the orders, she knew they couldn't afford the lost time or ingredients.

Carol walked in a few minutes later. "Harvey says he'll call back." She pulled out a rack of bare cupcakes and took them to the decorating area. "Once you get the guy's name, you should see if he has a social media presence. Most everyone does these days."

"I don't." Hamish clattered in, hauling reusable bags full of groceries. He hefted them up onto an empty table. "I can't imagine why people think everyone is interested in their business."

Molly laughed. "Judging from all the questions I had to deflect this morning, it appears everyone is interested."

"Check out the business site for Camden Landry and Nathan Glower's company," Laura suggested as she began unloading the grocery bags. "Maybe the guy is an employee."

Molly perked up at that idea. "Smart thinking. If Harvey can't get his name, I may find it on the company website. Either way, once I get these cookies done, I'm going to do some searching."

"As long as it's cookies first, sleuthing second," Laura said sternly.

Molly saluted. "Yes ma'am."

As it turned out, Molly finished two batches of the melting moments, both perfect, by the time Harvey called back. Carol positively glowed with pride at Harvey's success. "The man's name is Sid Loftis."

"Excellent," Molly said. "Then if you both will excuse me, I'm heading up to the office to do some research. I have the feeling this man is going to prove vital to understanding what's going on."

But Molly's bravado wavered slightly when she realized Harvey may have just given her the name of a cold-blooded killer.

12

Molly was greeted in the apartment by a cheery Angus who demanded a thorough petting before following her to the office and flopping at her feet. Molly absently rubbed his belly with the toe of one foot while she booted up the computer.

She began by searching for the software company by name, Prognostechnology. Their slogan—*We see the future of tech!*—didn't help her much in understanding what the company did. She continued clicking until she found an index of their products, mostly business software, along with a list of clients. The company appeared to be doing well.

From there, she clicked a tab that offered an opportunity to meet the company's leaders. As expected, it was a page of short bios with photographs. Molly quickly recognized both Camden Landry and Nathan Glower, both smiling confidently in their headshots. They were listed as founders and co-owners. There were also a few photos of other employees of the company, but Molly didn't see either Sid Loftis or Kaitlin Landry.

Since the site had a search bar, she put in Kaitlin Landry's name, but to no avail. She switched to a search engine and tried again. This brought up a few newspaper photos of the woman at various social events. Though the captions mentioned her by name, none connected her to Prognostechnology. However, it was clear that Kaitlin was on the board of several charities.

Molly then searched the charities by name and, after a brief tour of their websites, quickly found Prognostechnology listed as a patron for each one. How exactly was Kaitlin connected to the company? Was it only through being Camden's sister?

Frustrated, Molly called up the search engine again and typed in *Sid Loftis*. She found him on the site of a small software app company he owned called Lofty Goals. The apps it made were for mobile devices and targeted individual users rather than larger businesses. What could the man possibly have in common with Nathan Glower that would bring him to Loch Mallaig and lead to a heated argument?

Molly began to tap her foot as her frustration built, and Angus got up and moved a few feet away from her when her toe poked him lightly. "Sorry, buddy."

Angus didn't forgive her. He turned his back on her before curling up on the floor again. Molly finished her search on Sid Loftis by checking his company's address. It was in Milwaukee, the same as Prognostechnology.

Molly drummed her fingers on the table as she considered what to do next. She heard the sound of the apartment door opening and called, "I'm in the office."

Chloe poked her head in. "Mom," she scolded. "I thought you'd come and tell me about your visit with Nathan. I assume he's going to be okay."

"He seemed fine," Molly said. "Chloe, did you ever meet anyone named Sid Loftis?"

Molly shook her head. "I don't think so."

"He was at The Wandering when Nathan Glower was there. He's a stocky guy with glasses."

Chloe gaped at her mother in surprise. "I don't remember seeing Nathan Glower at The Wandering."

"You were walking Angus when they were there," Molly said. "Anyway, this Sid Loftis was arguing with Nathan at the Moose Lake

Country Club today. And he's staying at their lodge, according to someone on the housekeeping staff. That means he could have been the one to poison Nathan."

"But would he have been at the guesthouse when we met with Camden?" Chloe winced slightly, seeming to have trouble saying his name. "I would have thought that the person who poisoned Cam and the person who poisoned Nathan would be one and the same."

"It would be logical," Molly said. "It makes more sense than to imagine a bunch of poisoners running around Loch Mallaig. Not that anything has made a lot of sense in the past few days."

Chloe sank into a second chair in the small office. "Sorry, Mom. I feel like I brought a storm of trouble to Loch Mallaig. Though I don't know how."

"You didn't do anything wrong," Molly said. "Don't apologize."

"But I feel guilty," Chloe said. "And you even had to go talk to the police this morning. If anyone should be carted off to the police, it's me. I'm the one connected to everything."

"But I'm the one who chatted with Nathan before he collapsed," Molly said. "We're in this together, sweetheart." Then Molly gave her daughter a teasing grin. "So if we're off to jail, we can be cellmates."

"That would be good," Chloe said. "Then when Fergus arranges a jailbreak, he'll spring me too."

Molly laughed. "What makes you assume it would be Fergus who tried to break us out? I would think Laura and Carol would be first in line."

"They would definitely help," Chloe said. "But it's Fergus who would have the connections to pull it off."

At the absurd idea of a jailbreak involving any of her friends, Molly was reduced to giggles and Chloe joined in. They laughed long enough for Angus to sit up and bark at them, clearly wanting in on the fun.

"Now we've got Angus worked up," Molly said as the little terrier danced around the room.

"No worries," Chloe said. "I'll take him for a walk." When she stood up, Angus ran in circles around her feet, clearly sensing he was about to go on an adventure with one of his favorite people.

"Be good," Molly told him, but if the dog heard her, he gave no sign. "Thanks, Chloe. I'm going to finish my research, then I'll check for new online orders and get to work packing boxes."

"I'll join you after I run some of the energy out of this wild thing," Chloe replied.

Molly watched them fondly as they left the office together. If it hadn't been for the horror of Camden's death, she'd be having a perfect visit with her daughter. With a sigh, she refocused on the computer.

What to search for now? She knew there must be a rock or two she hadn't turned over. With a burst of inspiration, she typed Georgia Pinter's name into the search bar. Nothing useful came up right away, and Molly had to click through a number of references to people who clearly weren't the Georgia Pinter she wanted. Finally, she ended up at a social networking site, staring at the pale face and coal-black hair of the Georgia Pinter she knew.

Georgia's expression in the profile photo was solemn, even a bit haunted. Molly read over her page and saw she listed her relationship status as "complicated" and her location as Milwaukee.

Molly sucked in her breath. The coincidence of Georgia being from Milwaukee strained the limits of Molly's credulity. She thought about Myra telling her that Georgia and Kaitlin had hit it off and spent a lot of time together in the kitchen. Could that be because they'd known one another all along?

Molly began to flip through the photo gallery on Georgia's profile, hoping to find a photo containing any of the other people connected to Camden Landry. However, all the pictures the woman posted were selfies that included no other people.

With the photos offering nothing helpful, Molly began flipping through Georgia's feed. She found a series of posts about her relationship with a rich software developer, but Georgia didn't mention him or the company by name. Molly tapped the table and wondered if Georgia's relationship was with Sid Loftis or Nathan Glower. Had she come to Loch Mallaig at the behest of a rich software developer boyfriend?

Molly continued to skim posts for clues, then stared in shock at a reference Georgia made to her college days and something funny that had happened during her graduation from pharmacy school.

Pharmacy school? What would a pharmacist from Milwaukee be doing working as a waitress in Loch Mallaig? And more importantly, had her work as a pharmacist given Georgia access to the drugs that killed Camden and nearly killed Nathan?

Molly stared at Georgia Pinter's photo and wondered if she was seeing a murderer.

13

With her hand shaking so hard it was difficult to dial, Molly called the police station and asked to speak to Deputy Chief Gillespie. "I'm sorry," the polite voice on the phone said. "The deputy chief is not available. Would you care to leave a message?"

Molly pressed her lips together. What could she say? "Please tell the chief that Georgia Pinter graduated from pharmacy school."

The operator repeated her message. "Is that all?"

"Tell him he can call Molly Ferris if he has questions." After exchanging a few pleasantries, Molly hung up feeling vaguely unsatisfied, knowing that she would have preferred to talk to the deputy chief and gauge how seriously he took the information she'd shared.

She checked the system for new orders but found none, then shut down the computer and headed downstairs to help pack boxes for the orders they'd already processed. She could at least tell her friends about what she'd discovered as she worked.

To her surprise, she found Carol and Laura cleaning up. "We're done for the day?" Molly asked.

Laura laughed. "Don't feel bad, there will be plenty of work tomorrow, including lots of Thanksgiving pie and bread orders for local delivery." She grinned. "Hamish is positively giddy about the long list of stops."

Molly could understand that. Hamish owned a green 1955 Studebaker Speedster he affectionately called Nessie, and his appreciation for vintage vehicles extended to Bread on Arrival's similarly distinctive delivery car: a 1939 LaSalle hearse that had come with the house. Molly loved how well it marketed their business around town. Plus, it was an adventure to drive.

Molly raised a hand. "I will focus on the bakery tomorrow. I promise."

"Don't make promises you can't keep," Carol chided her gently. "If my Jenny were in Chloe's place, the bakery would simply have to wait. We understand, truly."

Laura grinned at her crookedly. "What Carol said, only without the offspring as an example. We do understand, Molly, and we love Chloe, so we want her to be safe too. If you can be here tomorrow, that's fantastic, but if you need to be somewhere else, we understand. Family first."

"Family first," Carol agreed.

As Carol and Laura came in for a group hug, Molly blinked away the tears in her eyes and thought, not for the first time, that she had the best friends and business partners on the planet.

Laura broke the hug first. "Enough mushy stuff. I'm going home to put my feet up. I'll see you both in the morning." She spun and headed out of the kitchen with the brisk efficiency that only Laura could manage.

Carol gave Molly one last squeeze. "I need to get home and feed some chickens. Harvey thinks they're conspiring against him. Apparently they've been getting quiet when he comes into the coop. He says they're starting to figure out what happens to the eggs and he expects an uprising at any moment."

"I think Harvey may have missed his calling," Molly said with a chuckle. "He should have been writing novels. *The Great Chicken Revolt*. I'd read that."

"I don't have to read it. I live it, apparently." Carol shrugged into her coat. "I'll see you in the morning. Call if you need anything."

"I will," Molly promised.

As Carol headed for the back door, Chloe and Angus were coming in. They had another round of goodbyes before Carol finally left for the night.

"It's getting seriously cold out," Chloe told Molly as she reached down to unclip Angus's leash. "I was starting to wish I had Angus's fur coat. He wasn't bothered at all."

"I've seen him dive into the middle of a snowdrift for the fun of it," Molly told her as they followed Angus, who was taking advantage of the rare opportunity to wander around downstairs. "Did you have a nice walk, beyond the freezing part?"

"I did. Loch Mallaig is a beautiful town and I meet pleasant people everywhere I go," Chloe said. "Though I did see the grumpy librarian, and she glared at me like I was smuggling overdue library books."

"Grizela can be intimidating," Molly agreed. "But I think she has a good heart." Unfortunately, Molly remembered how staunchly the librarian had opposed The Wandering. Molly had mostly forgotten about the vandalism in light of the more serious happenings, but she couldn't help but wonder if it may have been related to The Wandering protests. There had been no more vandalism since the event, which made it all the more suspiciously linked in her mind.

"Mom, I can practically see the wheels spinning in your head," Chloe said. "What are you thinking about?"

"Nothing important," Molly answered, then noticed the expression on Chloe's face that usually indicated she was going to ask for a favor. "What do you need, honey?"

"You know me too well." Chloe bit her lip. "Since you're on friendly terms with Nathan, do you think you could find out when Cam's funeral will be? I assume it'll take place in Milwaukee. I want to attend if possible."

"Of course you do," Molly said. "I was actually thinking I would drive over to the Moose Lake Country Club. If I can catch Peggy Webster, I have some more questions. I'll ask about the funeral if I see Nathan."

"Okay. Hey, can I borrow that book you were reading? It sounded interesting and since I have time on my hands . . ."

"Sure, go ahead." Molly waved a hand. "But I warn you, it's scary."

"I love a good scary book." Chloe whistled for Angus, who rushed to them and followed Chloe up the stairs.

Molly grabbed her coat and headed out in the late afternoon gloom.

Ten minutes later, she pulled into the country club's parking lot and chose a spot close to the front door, one of the ones with a clear time limit printed on the sign. She didn't intend to be long, though she doubted anyone cared much this time of year.

She hopped out of her car, then spotted Peggy coming out one of the doors farthest from where she'd parked. Despite the distance, Molly could recognize her red curls anywhere, especially when they were unbound and frizzing into a lion's mane in the damp air. She trotted toward her. "Peggy!"

Peggy spun around, her face a mix of surprise and worry. The expression relaxed only slightly when she recognized Molly. A weak smile darted on to her face before falling away, and she stopped walking and waited for Molly.

"I wanted to ask you something," Molly said as she reached her.

Peggy winced. "I can't talk about guests."

"It's not about a guest—honest," Molly replied. "I was wondering if the country club had interviewed or hired a new employee. A pale woman with black hair? Her name is Georgia Pinter."

Peggy shook her head. "The country club isn't adding new staff. They're scaling back. They always do this time of year."

"You're sure?"

"If they've hired anyone, that would be the talk of the staff," Peggy said. "It's unheard of this time of year."

Molly sighed. She'd been aware it was a long shot, but if Georgia Pinter was at the center of the poisoning, she could have plans to try again since Nathan had survived the first time. Getting a job at the country club would have given her easy access to make another attempt.

"Have you seen anyone around like the woman I described?" Molly asked. "Her skin is unusually pale, and it's striking with the coal-black hair."

Peggy thought about it, then shook her head. "I haven't seen anyone like that." She frowned, then seemed to come to a conclusion. "I could ask around if you want. The staff does gossip a little. If anyone has seen her, I could tell you."

"That would be a huge help. Thank you."

Peggy's lips twitched upward. "That's okay. As long as it's not about a guest, I don't mind helping." She shivered. "I should be going. It's too cold out here for me."

"Of course," Molly said. "Sorry to hold you up. Thanks for your help."

Peggy bobbed her head and rushed off.

Molly remained where she was, trying to plan her next move. She wasn't enjoying standing out in the cold any more than Peggy had. In fact, a sudden icy breeze felt as if it slipped right down the collar of her jacket, making her shiver. *A cup of hot chocolate would warm me up.*

She hurried to the main entrance and was relieved to step into the well-heated lobby. The inside entrance to the lodge's restaurant, Mulligans, sported a sign with the evening specials. Mulligans was a casual spot, and the food was good.

As Molly stepped into the soft lighting of the restaurant, she paused to let her eyes adjust before approaching the hostess stand.

"Are you here to see me?"

Molly glanced around to find Nathan standing behind her. He was a little pale, but otherwise appeared to be fine, though Molly found it odd to see him in jeans and a light sweater. She'd come to associate him with suits.

"I was actually here to talk to a friend from church," she said. "But it's nice to see you. How are you feeling?"

"Famished," he said. "Would you care to join me for an early dinner?"

"I'll be eating at home with my daughter," Molly replied. "But I was thinking I'd enjoy a cup of hot chocolate to fortify me against the cold. I could sit with you a bit while I drink it."

"Sounds great." He herded her forward and asked the hostess for a table for two. The young woman behind the hostess stand must have recognized Molly, as she glanced from Molly to Nathan with interest before leading them to a table.

At the early hour, they had their choice of seats. Molly was glad they would be able to chat in relative privacy. Once they were settled and a waitress had taken their beverage order, Molly chatted a bit aimlessly until she thought of a question relevant to the strange things going on. "About that tray that was delivered by room service," she began. "You said the person spoke to you through the door. Was it a man or a woman?"

"A man," Nathan said. "But I couldn't tell you who. I haven't paid a lot of attention to the staff here, though they're all quite nice."

"Most people in Loch Mallaig are," Molly said. She was glad of the arrival of the waitress with her hot chocolate, as it gave her a moment to think of what to ask next. She took a warming sip from the mug, then set it carefully on the table in front of her. "Do you know who is staying in the rooms on either side of you?"

"Actually, an associate of mine, Sid Loftis, is in one room. Our company does business with his. You may have met him. He came to The Wandering event." He chuckled. "Though I'm sure you met a lot of people that night."

"And most didn't introduce themselves by name," Molly said. "I met you that night, but didn't learn your name until later."

"Right. Anyway, I am fairly sure Sid doesn't want to poison me," Nathan said with a smile.

Molly raised her mug. "So you're on good terms?" She sipped her hot chocolate, watching him carefully over the rim of the mug.

"As good as business allows," Nathan said. "Sid's the creative type, same as Cam." His face fell. "I still can't believe Cam is dead. I keep expecting to get a text or call from him. It's going to be surreal when I get to the office and he's not there."

"I'm sorry," Molly said. "That must be hard. When will the funeral be?"

Nathan shook his head. "Not until after the police let us leave, and that's up in the air. I should ask Kaitlin about it. She may need some help."

"It must be a difficult time for her," Molly said sympathetically. Though she didn't particularly care for the woman, she couldn't help but be sorry for her loss.

"I feel awful," he said. "I haven't called her to check in, and I should have."

"In your defense, you were in the hospital."

Nathan gazed at her approvingly. "You're a good person, Molly Ferris. You'd make a great bartender. I feel as if I could pour out all my woes to you."

Molly felt her face warm under the compliment. Mildly uncomfortable under Nathan's admiring gaze, she changed the subject. "So Sid is in one of the rooms next to yours. Have you noticed who is in the other one?"

Nathan chuckled. "You'd make a great detective too. Always on the case. Okay, Detective Ferris, let me think. I thought the room next to me was empty. I never saw anyone come in or out, and it was very quiet on that side. Though the walls here are pretty thick. But this afternoon, I saw that I have a neighbor, a woman."

"What does she look like?"

"Thin."

"That's all you noticed?" Molly asked. "Not hair color or age?"

"I only saw her for a split second," he said. "She ducked into her room quickly as I was coming out. And she was wearing a knit cap so I couldn't see her hair. The hat was gray, if that helps. But otherwise, I wasn't really paying attention."

And that meant the woman next door to Nathan could be either Kaitlin or Georgia. They were both thin, and if the woman had plans to harm Nathan, she wouldn't want him to see her. Maybe she had ducked in quickly to keep Nathan from recognizing her.

"I think you should be careful of anything you eat or drink in the days ahead," Molly said finally. "Whoever tried to hurt you may not be done."

"Don't worry," he said. "I intend to be extremely careful." He picked up the coffee mug the waitress had left for him and gazed into it pensively before meeting Molly's gaze. "Not to be a doomsayer, but it occurs to me that whoever is poisoning people wouldn't appreciate it if they found out you're asking questions. You may need to be careful of what you eat or drink as well."

With a shiver, Molly realized he was probably right.

14

Early Wednesday morning, Molly crept downstairs while Chloe slept, determined to make up for her recent time away from the bakery. She suspected they'd be busy with folks dashing in to purchase last-minute Thanksgiving breads and desserts since the holiday was the next day.

The soft glow of the hallway light cast monstrous shadows near the large kitchen's tables and appliances. Though not normally afraid of the dark, Molly quickly groped for the switch near the doorway. The past few days had made her appreciate the way the light transformed the kitchen into the warm, friendly place she loved.

She picked up the list of orders to find something she could work on alone, mentally crossing out anything that required a particularly complex recipe or advanced technique. Then her gaze landed on an item she'd made dozens of times. "Bingo!"

By the time Carol and Laura came in, Molly was mixing a batch of pumpkin custard to fill a batch of pie shells Carol had whipped up the day before.

"It smells like Thanksgiving in here already," Carol said as she shrugged out of her thick jacket. "I love that smell."

Before she could hang up the jacket, Laura picked a piece of hay from the sleeve. "New accessory?"

Carol shrugged. "Had to feed the girls before I left the house."

"You're hardier than I." Laura gave a mock shiver. "I prefer to feed hungry mouths from the warmth of this kitchen."

Molly smiled at her friends. She knew they were only teasing. In fact, she'd once seen Laura petting one of Carol's hens. Molly had to agree that it was hard to resist touching the soft feathers of the friendly birds. "I like the chickens," she said. "But I love being warm too."

"The trip to the coop is harder some days than others," Carol conceded as she headed for the cooler, drying her hands on her apron. "I'll pull the shells I made yesterday and pop them in to blind bake."

"They're already in," Molly said, pointing with her spoon. "That's the timer for them."

"Wow, you have been a busy little bee this morning," Carol said admiringly. "So what did you leave for me?"

"Everything harder than pumpkin pie," Molly told her with a laugh.

Laura checked her list. "There are some pumpkin rolls for early pickup, if you don't mind getting those, Carol. You are the cake maven, after all. I'll tackle the apple pies."

For a long while, the kitchen bustled with minimal chatting. They had a lot to accomplish, and they all felt the pressure. They barely paused when Hamish and Bridget buzzed through the kitchen to clock in before heading out front to prepare for opening.

Everyone was so focused on the tasks at hand that Molly yelped when she heard her phone and nearly dropped the pan of buttery dinner rolls she was retrieving from the oven at the time. She slid the pan into a cooling rack, then pulled her phone from her pocket and checked the display. "It's someone from the police station." She answered with no small amount of trepidation.

"Sorry to call this early," Greer said, "but I know you keep baker's hours."

"That's true," Molly agreed as she stepped out into the hall to hear better, away from the sounds of the kitchen. She felt slight relief at hearing a friendly voice on the other end of the line, especially since she'd texted Greer the tip about Nathan having a suspicious neighbor. Maybe she was calling about that.

Sure enough, Greer said, "I'll be brief. We checked out your hunch about Georgia having the room next to Nathan. Apparently she did check into the room on the same day that Nathan checked in, though none of the housekeeping staff saw personal items in the room at any time. She's still checked in, but the room is empty. No belongings at all."

"So it's probably not where she's actually staying," Molly said.

"No, but why is she paying for a room that she isn't using? Moose Lake Country Club is no Castleglen, but it's not cheap either."

"What if she only checked in to watch for a chance to poison Nathan?"

"That's not a bad theory, but we can't find any clear connection between Georgia and Nathan Glower, nor Georgia and Camden Landry, other than all of them being from Milwaukee."

"I saw a social networking page for Georgia," Molly said. "She made reference in one post to a boyfriend at a software company. What if Georgia dated Camden and received the same treatment as Chloe? She'd have reason to be mad at Nathan for that."

"But mad enough to poison two people?" Greer asked.

"It's possible. We're not sure who was the intended target of the first poisoning," Molly said. "If Camden had dated Georgia in the past, he could have seen her at the guesthouse and told her why he was in town, not realizing she might see Chloe as competition that needed to be eliminated."

"That sounds a bit fanciful," Greer said. "I'm not saying I'll discard the possibility, but it is a stretch."

"Perhaps," Molly admitted, "but something strange is going on with Georgia. She rented an expensive room where she apparently never stayed. It put her in position to poison Nathan. She fixed the tea that poisoned Camden. And the Loganachs reported that she spent a lot of time in the kitchen chatting with Kaitlin. Right now, Georgia is the one person we know interacted with everyone in the case."

"It's certainly strange, but the motives are shallow."

"Well, if it's not Georgia, then it must be one of the other people from Milwaukee," Molly said. "No one in Loch Mallaig had reason to kill any of them."

"True," Greer said, but something in her tone made Molly feel there was something the officer wasn't saying, and Molly suspected she knew what it was.

Chloe was also from Milwaukee.

"Chloe didn't hurt anyone," Molly insisted.

"I believe you," Greer said, and this time she sounded completely sincere. "Molly, I promise we're examining all of these people. Please leave the investigation to us and enjoy your Thanksgiving."

Molly murmured something mildly agreeable and ended the call, feeling as if she hadn't gotten anywhere. As far as she was concerned, Georgia was the prime suspect, and finding her should be a priority. Once they located the woman, they could try to determine the motive. At least Molly hoped so.

When she turned to the kitchen, she found Chloe had slipped by her while she was completely focused on her phone call.

"Mom, you should have woken me," her daughter scolded. "I wanted to help out today."

"No worries," Laura sang out. "We have plenty to do. In fact, if you want to jump in, Chloe, you can unload that rack and slip all the loaves of bread into paper sleeves to go on the display up front."

"I'm on it," Chloe said with a crisp salute.

"So tell us," Carol interjected. "What did the police want?"

"Police?" Chloe yelped, stopping in the middle of reaching for a cooled tray of bread. "Do we have to go in again?"

"Not this time," Molly reassured her daughter. "Greer was just updating me." While they all got back to work, Molly explained about Georgia Pinter having a room at the country club while purportedly staying at the guesthouse. "And now no one can say where she is, but she had the ability to poison Nathan's coffee and your tea."

"But why would she do that?" Chloe asked, shoving a loaf hard enough to tear the paper sleeve. "She was nice on the night of The Wandering. I thought we got along. And I didn't know her in Milwaukee."

"I think she may have known Camden," Molly said gently as she handed Chloe a fresh paper sleeve. "Nathan told me he's interfered in Camden's relationships more than once. I think one of those relationships could have been with Georgia. She could have been angry about it."

"I was angry about it," Chloe said. "But not enough to kill someone. That's not a reasonable response."

"People don't always respond reasonably," Molly replied.

Chloe shook her head. "I appreciate that you have given this some thought, Mom, but I can't see it. Even if she wanted to hurt Nathan, she'd have no reason to hurt me. I felt she and I could be friends."

"Unless she was hoping to get Camden back, and you stood in the way," Molly suggested.

"We have no idea that she even knew Camden," Chloe said, her voice rising from exasperation. "I think your theory has wandered pretty far into the weeds, Mom." Then she held up her hand. "Can we put this whole investigation or whatever on hold? I could use a nice, normal Thanksgiving." She pushed the last loaf of bread into a paper sleeve. "If it's okay, I think I'll take Angus for a walk and clear my head."

"Of course," Laura told her, giving Molly a mildly reproving glance.

"Sorry, sweetheart," Molly said. "Have a nice walk. I think it's going to be a pretty day."

"Pretty cold," Carol said. "Be sure to put on a coat."

"I will." Chloe laughed. "I love spending Thanksgiving here, but it's a little like having three moms."

Carol gave her a sideways hug. "Lucky you."

"Right," Chloe said, drawing the word out. "Lucky me."

Molly gave her friends a sheepish grin after Chloe left. "I was insensitive, wasn't I?"

"She did just lose a friend," Laura said.

Molly let the grin drop. "I'll have to apologize."

"And she'll forgive you," Carol said. "That's how mother-daughter relationships work. Someone is always in need of apologizing for something."

With that, the conversation drifted to Thanksgiving and the order sheet, which kept everyone motivated for a bit. As Molly finished boxing up some special order pumpkin pies and tagging them with customer names, she heard a knock on the back door. "Chloe must be back," she said.

When she reached the door, she was surprised to find Grizela on the stoop, her hand on the arm of a teenage boy. The boy was at the gangly age where a growth spurt had left him awkward in his own body. The slightly short sleeves on his jacket added to the impression. Other than his red hair, partially covered by a knit cap, Molly couldn't see much of the boy's face since he hung his head.

The librarian's shrewd green eyes glinted sharply as she tugged the boy's arm. "Molly," she said firmly, "young Austin here has something to say to you, Carol, and Laura."

Without looking up, the young man mumbled something Molly couldn't understand.

"Hold on," Grizela said, giving the young man's arm another shake. "You'll need to say it to all three of them. You might as well do it at one time. May we come in?"

"Of course," Molly said. *As if I could keep Grizela Duff from doing anything.* She backed away from the door, and Grizela prodded the young man through.

Grizela and Austin preceded Molly into the kitchen, where the librarian announced to a surprised Laura and Carol that Austin had something to tell them. She poked him. "Loud enough to be heard."

The boy raised his eyes for the briefest of moments before saying directly at the floor, "I'm sorry for vandalizing your property. I shouldn't have done it. And I'll be happy to work and make it up."

The apology and offer of reparations had a slightly rote quality to it, and Molly was sure Grizela had gone over exactly what he should say.

"It's good of you to confess, Austin," Laura said as she laced her fingers together. "We did have to pay to have the paint removed. We'd be glad to get that money reimbursed."

The teenager swallowed visibly and raised his eyes to Laura. "I'll pay with the money I made raking leaves."

"Austin," Carol said gently, "why on earth did you do it?"

Grizela cleared her throat. "That is partly my fault."

The shock of having Grizela take the blame for anything drew every gaze toward her. Molly nearly gaped as she saw the older woman's cheeks redden.

"Austin is a volunteer at the library," Grizela explained. "I wasn't happy about The Wandering, as you are aware. And I may have spoken strongly about it in front of Austin. I didn't realize he would want to do something about it, but I should have been more diplomatic about my disapproval."

"You were fired up about it," Carol said, her tone mildly amused. "We all knew that."

"But speaking of fire," Molly said. "As messy and expensive as it was to fix the paint, the fire was worse. We're lucky it didn't spread beyond the pail."

"Fire?" Grizela repeated as she glared at Austin. "You didn't say anything about a fire."

Austin glanced from face to face, his eyes wide. "I didn't start any fire. I promise. I threw the paint, but I made sure the can said it would wash off. I wouldn't start a fire. That's dangerous." His voice was so urgent that Molly felt sure he was speaking the truth.

"Okay, Austin," Carol said. "We believe you."

The teenager's shoulders relaxed, and he almost smiled. "Thanks."

Laura told him the amount they'd paid Kelvin Mooney to wash off the paint, and Austin promised to bring the money before the bakery closed for the day. Grizela finally switched from prodding the teenager with her bony finger to patting him approvingly on the shoulder.

"We're still short one prankster," Laura said after Grizela and Austin had left.

"If Grizela was ranting about us in front of a lot of people, it could have been a different library volunteer, or even a patron," Carol suggested. "Clearly she was inspirational for mischief makers."

"Well, I suppose we should put it behind us," Molly said. "We may never find out." Though she didn't say it, she thought perhaps the fire hadn't been connected to The Wandering at all, nor to Grizela's rants. It could have been another attempt to hurt Chloe, after all. The fire could easily have caught the old building and done serious damage.

Molly had barely begun boxing pies before another knock sounded at the back door. "This time, it's sure to be Chloe," she said.

When she pulled open the back door, she found the last person Molly would have expected to see.

Georgia Pinter stood on the stoop with her hands shoved in the pockets of a thick gray hoodie. A thatch of her coal-black hair showed under the hood, and her pale face was pink and angry.

Molly recoiled from the woman's furious face and had a fleeting thought. *She looks mad enough to kill.*

15

Georgia pulled one hand out of her hoodie pocket and jabbed it at Molly. "What do you think you're doing?" she hissed. "Why are you trying to pin a murder on me?"

"I'm not trying to pin a murder on anyone," Molly said. She gestured toward the door. "Why don't you come in? You can have some coffee, and we'll talk about it."

Georgia shook her head vehemently enough that it made her hood slide off her head, letting more of her dark hair fall into her face. "I'm not going in there. And I'm not a killer."

"I didn't say you were," Molly insisted as she stepped through the door to stand on the back porch with Georgia, closing the door behind her. "But you have to realize your actions are suspicious. You brought the tea to our table. The tea was laced with drugs that would be easy for a pharmacist to get."

Georgia froze in the process of pulling her hood up again and her eyes narrowed. "What are you trying to say?"

"That you had the opportunity and you had the means." Molly folded her arms over her chest. "Plus, when Nathan was poisoned by drugs in his coffee, you were the person who rented the room beside his. Who else had access to both?"

Georgia stared at her. "What are you talking about?"

Molly dropped her firm stance as she wondered if Georgia was going to continue to plead ignorance. "Why were you working at the Two Scots Guesthouse?"

Georgia shifted her feet. "I can't say." Then she perked up. "But I wasn't alone in the kitchen. Kaitlin was there with me. She would have seen if I'd put anything in the tea. Has anyone asked her?"

Molly wondered if anyone had asked Kaitlin about her friendship with Georgia. She assumed the police had, but they didn't tell her everything they knew. "That's an odd friendship," she said instead. "You and Kaitlin."

Georgia shrugged. "Kaitlin is nice enough once you spend time with her. She can be passionate about some things, sure, but she's not a bad person. And she was only in Loch Mallaig to help her brother."

"Help him?" Molly echoed.

"Kaitlin said her brother is a great guy and smart about everything except women. He had dated questionable women before, and when Kaitlin found out he'd come to town to reconnect with someone, she rushed here."

"My daughter is not a questionable woman," Molly said firmly.

Georgia's expression grew sheepish. "Once I met her, I didn't think so either. I tried to tell Kaitlin she was wrong about Chloe, but Kaitlin isn't someone who changes her mind easily once it's made up. And I guess she had some reason, some woman in Camden's past."

"Were you one of the women in Camden's past?" Molly asked.

Georgia gaped at her, then burst into laughter. "No way," she said. "Wow, is that a miss. No, Camden Landry wasn't ever my boyfriend. I met him once, but that's about it. You need to rethink your sources, Molly Ferris."

Molly folded her arms over her chest again, though it was as much for the cold creeping through her light sweater as anything else. "One of my sources was your social media. You had a post about your boyfriend, and the description could have been Camden."

Georgia stared blankly, clearly bewildered. "I don't remember the post, but I promise it wasn't Camden. And keep in mind, I wasn't alone in the kitchen, so I couldn't have poisoned anyone. I had no reason to do that. I didn't have bad feelings about Camden Landry or anyone else."

"Fine, I had it wrong," Molly said. "So set me straight. I ask again, why are you in Loch Mallaig? If you want me to be on your side, I need the truth."

Georgia's grin faded. She shoved her hands in her pockets and shifted on her feet again. She seemed to be weighing how much to tell Molly. Before she came to a conclusion, the door behind Molly rattled, making her whirl around.

The door opened, and Hamish stuck his head out. He blinked rapidly as a sharp, cold breeze blew right in his face. With a hand over his squinted eyes, he said, "Laura sent me to find out what's keeping you out in the cold."

"I'm talking," Molly said, shivering. The same chill breeze felt as if it had frozen her neck.

Hamish made a big show of looking around. "Talking with whom?"

Molly spun again. The back porch and surrounding area were empty. There was no sign of Georgia Pinter at all. "She was right there. You must have seen her."

"I dinnae see anyone, but with the wind in my face, I wouldn't have. I'm sure someone was here," Hamish said, though Molly thought his tone sounded a bit too agreeable, as if he was humoring her. "Why don't you come in and warm up, lass?"

"Mom!"

Molly and Hamish both spun to see Chloe half-dragged across the leaf-strewn lawn by an eager Angus. Though the Scottish terrier was a small dog, he was more than willing to throw his full weight into getting where he wanted to go—and right now, he wanted to get to Hamish.

Though Hamish pretended to be indifferent to the little dog, Molly knew the older man secretly adored her dog as much as Angus adored him.

"You'd best take care, lass," Hamish said to Chloe, his tone gruff. "That wee ruffian will keep you out in the cold until your fingers freeze off."

"He does love to walk," Chloe agreed as Angus rushed up the porch steps to dance around Hamish's feet. Chloe frowned at Molly. "Were you hunting for me? And where's your coat? You'd nag me into next week for being out here without mine."

"I wasn't expecting to be out here," Molly said defensively. "I had answered a knock at the door, and then I was out here talking to Georgia Pinter. Did you see her?"

Chloe shook her head. "No. Is she okay?"

"She's fine for now, but she's harboring secrets." Molly sighed. "She apparently took off when she heard the back door opening. If you run into her, don't go anywhere alone with her."

"Och," Hamish said. "Am I hearing Molly Ferris caution someone against rash behavior?" Molly made a face at him, but Hamish paid her no mind. "If you two are committed to standing out in the cold, let me take Angus off your hands before he chews off one of my shoelaces."

Chloe handed Hamish the leash and faced her mother directly. "Mom, I'm not sure I'm the one we should be worried about."

"What do you mean?" Molly asked as she followed Hamish inside, eager to step out of the cold.

Chloe stopped her in the hall with a hand on her arm. "Well, if Georgia didn't kill Camden—and I don't think she did—then someone else out there is a killer. And you said she seemed to know more than she was saying. Plus, she ran off when she heard the door."

"All right," Molly agreed, rubbing her chilled arms.

"So Georgia is in hiding," Chloe said as she pulled off her gloves and shoved them in the pockets of her coat.

"I assume she's hiding from the police," Molly told her. "They certainly want to speak with her."

Chloe shrugged out of her coat and folded it over her arm. "But that isn't all. If Georgia knows who killed Camden, then she could be in serious danger. She has a secret somebody doesn't want the world to find out."

Molly mulled that over, nodding slowly. "If Georgia is in danger, then we'd better find her before the danger comes to pass."

"Do you have any ideas as to how we'd do that?"

Molly didn't. She took Chloe's coat and carried it to the row of hooks. "She may have met local people while she worked at the guesthouse. I suppose someone might have taken her in." Then her eyes widened as she thought of one person who was already Georgia's friend. "Or maybe someone from Milwaukee is helping hide her."

"Who?" Chloe asked.

"I have an idea, but I want to run it by Laura and Carol," Molly said. "Besides, I should get back to helping. Let's go do some brainstorming together."

As Molly and Chloe walked into the kitchen, Laura glanced up from decoratively docking the tops of several apple pies with perfectly fluted edges. "I wondered if you were going to stay outside until you froze."

"It is chilly out," Molly agreed. "But I was talking to Georgia Pinter."

Laura and Carol both stared at Molly through wide, surprised eyes. "And you stood chatting with her in a spot no one else could see,"

Carol said reproachfully. "You take way too many risks sometimes. What if she had attacked you?"

"Then Mom would have hollered, and you all would have come running. Besides, I don't think Georgia is that kind of person," Chloe said.

Molly pushed up her sweater sleeves. "I can't say that I believe in her quite as much as Chloe does, but I'm beginning to see Georgia in a different light. She said she never dated Camden, for one thing. And from her surprise at my assumption, I believe her."

"That doesn't necessarily mean she had nothing to do with his poisoning," Laura said.

Molly walked over to help Carol fill cookie boxes. "Georgia said Kaitlin was in the kitchen with her when she fixed the tea for Chloe and me. Apparently Kaitlin can testify that Georgia never tampered with the tea."

"Then why didn't the police say that?" Laura asked as she carried a pie to the oven.

"That's a good question for me to ask Greer," Molly said, realizing it led her to another thought. "What if I've been suspecting Georgia when Kaitlin was to blame all the time?"

Chloe gasped. "You think Kaitlin poisoned her brother? What kind of horrible person would do that?"

Molly shook her head. "I think Kaitlin tried to poison you, or you and me. I don't think she ever intended Camden to drink the tea."

Chloe's face paled. "But why poison us?"

"To protect her brother," Molly said. "Or his money. Georgia wouldn't tell me why she was in Loch Mallaig, but what if Kaitlin asked her to come to help her with her plot? While Georgia was watching Camden, Kaitlin could be free to eliminate the woman that Camden hoped to date again."

"Or," Laura said as she picked up a second apple pie and headed to the oven, "Georgia could have lied to you. After all, she was at the guesthouse under suspicious circumstances. If she did kill Camden, then lying probably came with the murderer package."

"Plus, none of this explains why Georgia has a room at the Moose Lake Country Club that she doesn't appear to be using," Carol added. Leaving Molly to fill the cookie boxes, she gathered an armload of crusty loaves from the day-old rack and carried them to another table. She motioned for Chloe to join her, and together they began cutting the loaves into small cubes for Thanksgiving dressing.

"I don't think Georgia is guilty of hurting anyone," Chloe said stubbornly as she sawed at the bread.

"Georgia was weird when I asked her about the country club," Molly mused. "She was surprised by the question."

Chloe gestured with the knife. "Maybe she didn't make the reservation."

Carol gently lowered Chloe's hand and the knife back to the bread. "Or she was surprised that Molly knew about it."

"I need to talk to Georgia some more," Molly said. "But that means figuring out where she is. And I could only come up with one person who might know."

"Kaitlin," Laura and Carol said in unison.

"That's exactly what I was thinking," Molly said. "If anybody can tell us where Georgia is, it's Kaitlin."

"But Kaitlin isn't going to tell any of us," Laura argued. "None of us have had any positive interactions with the woman."

"That's true," Molly said glumly. "But there is one thing I have to do now."

"What's that?" Chloe asked.

"Go down to the police station and tell them about my encounter with Georgia." Molly closed the lid on the cookie box she'd just filled. "Whatever we may think, they're searching for her. And it'll look bad if I don't tell them she was here."

"I still say she's innocent," Chloe said loyally.

"I'll tell them that too, but Georgia needs to come clean if she wants them to believe it." Molly groaned. "I'm not at all sure they're going to be happy to speak to me."

"You could call instead," Laura suggested.

"It's tempting, but I want to be able to judge their reaction when I tell them," Molly said. "And that's best done face-to-face. But don't worry. I'm not budging until we get every item checked off the things-to-do list."

Laura grinned at her. "In that case, you have my complete support."

16

By midday, Laura's list was complete, though new orders continued to come in by phone. Molly tackled each new item without comment, but she was feeling antsy. She wanted to be able to put her focus on Thanksgiving when morning dawned, and she knew she wouldn't be able to do that without making her trip to the police station.

Laura walked into the kitchen from the customer area, leafing through the most recent orders. "Clearly orders are going to come in until we close."

Carol paused in wiping down one of the workstations. "That's optimistic. I bet we'll be getting last-minute calls after that too."

Molly suspected her friend was right. She gave her friend a brave smile. "Don't worry. I'm all in."

"Me too," Chloe sang out. "Well, after lunch. I'm starving."

"All volunteer workers should feel comfortable coming and going as you please," Carol said as she rinsed her cloth in the sink. "I brought a sandwich from home, so I won't need much of a break."

"I brought a salad," Laura told her. "So I'll join you." Then she pointed the wad of papers at Molly. "You, on the other hand, should go to the police station and tell them about Georgia. We'll be fine."

"And take something to eat," Carol said. "Don't skip lunch. You'll have more trouble keeping up when you get back."

Molly smiled at her friend's motherly advice. "I'll take a scone along. And I promise not to dawdle."

At the police station, Molly brushed a scone crumb from the front of her coat and approached the reception desk. She swallowed a groan as Wilma Guthrie's face lit up at the sight of her.

Wilma dropped her voice to a loud whisper and leaned forward. "Do you have some new information on the murder?"

Molly knew that anything she said in front of Wilma was on the fast track to every ear in Loch Mallaig. As a result, she spoke hesitantly. "I came to talk with Officer Anderson, if she's available."

Disappointment washed over Wilma's face. "About The Piping Yoopers?"

Molly considered simply agreeing. It would be a lie, and Molly tried hard to tell as few of those as possible, but it would certainly make her life easier. Finally, she decided to sidestep the question altogether. "Is Greer around?"

"She's in a meeting with the deputy chief right now," Wilma went on in her stage whisper. "If you want to take a seat, I'll tell her you need a word."

"Thank you, Wilma."

Molly headed for the row of chairs meant for visitors and was surprised to see Sid Loftis in one of them. She walked over and sat near the man. "I think we met at The Wandering," she said. "I co-own the bakehouse."

The man blinked at her behind his glasses, then smiled. "Right, I remember. The tart I had was fantastic. Do you have more of those at the bakery? I should stop by."

"I expect we have a few, though business is booming today with Thanksgiving tomorrow."

At the mention of the holiday, the man's face fell. "This is going to be the first Thanksgiving I've missed at my mom's house. She lives in Milwaukee."

"You're a long way from home," Molly said.

He shifted in the chair. "It's for work. I hope it'll be worth it."

Molly waved a hand. "I hope you're not here to report anything unfortunate happening to you. I'd hate for your time in Loch Mallaig to be a negative."

"No, everyone has been really nice," he said. "If my work and family weren't in Milwaukee, I wouldn't mind living in a little town like this. It's pretty. I'm here because someone died. I didn't know the man, but I'm sort of connected with his business. I doubt I can help much."

"It's good of you to come in," Molly said. "It's not the nicest way to spend the day before Thanksgiving. I think they're holding a dinner at the Moose Lake Country Club tomorrow. It won't be home, but at least you can get some turkey and mashed potatoes."

"I'm staying there, so I've seen the signs for it." He leaned toward her. "It's a little spooky. I think we're the only people there."

"We?" Molly repeated. "So you won't be totally alone for Thanksgiving?"

"We haven't talked about it," he said. "It's business. See I'm a software designer, and I opened a small company. But this bigger operation wants to hire me, which will effectively mean folding my business into theirs. It's a big step, but it would be more money and more contacts."

"And this bigger company is here in Michigan?"

"No. That's what makes it dopey. The company is located in Milwaukee too, but one of the bigwigs wanted me to meet with another of the bigwigs, and he was here in Loch Mallaig. It's ridiculously convoluted. I should have insisted on staying in Milwaukee."

Molly observed the man's frustrated expression. She wondered if his argument with Nathan had something to do with his desire to be home for Thanksgiving. "Have you considered simply leaving?"

"I did. Yesterday, I even told the guy I was leaving. He was none too happy, but what could he do? But then I got a call from the police." Sid sighed deeply. "I should be home. My twin sister is pregnant with her second child. She's due any day, and I'm supposed to babysit my nephew while Meg is in the hospital. What will she do if she goes into labor before I can get home?"

"Hopefully, you won't be tied up here much longer," Molly said sympathetically. "Maybe they'll even let you leave after you talk to the police today."

"That would be great," Sid said.

"This bigwig you talked about—is it the man you were with at The Wandering?"

"Same guy," Sid said. "Nathan Glower."

"But you never met the other bigwig?"

He shook his head. "Nathan said he wasn't normally involved with hiring people. I did meet his sister at their office in Milwaukee. She's nice enough. She's supposed to be here in Loch Mallaig too, though I haven't seen her." He slumped slightly.

Molly felt bad for Sid. She didn't think he was a bad guy, and she now understood why he had argued with Nathan. *If Sid is telling the truth, that is.* Then she had a thought. Sid was in the software business. "Have you ever met Georgia Pinter?"

His expression grew suspicious. "Why?"

"She's from Milwaukee too," Molly said. "She's a pharmacist."

Sid's suspicious expression changed to one of amusement. "Do you have any idea how many people live in Milwaukee? It's not like Loch Mallaig. People don't all know each other."

That didn't answer her question. She started to ask him again, but they were interrupted when Wilma called out Sid's name. "Mr. Loftis? They'll see you now."

Sid gave Molly a last nod. "Nice to meet you. If I get out of here in time, I'll stop by the bakery and buy myself a pick-me-up tart."

"We have some good ones," Molly said. "I hope you get home soon."

"You and me both."

Molly watched him disappear into the back. She wondered about Nathan's hiring of Sid. Wasn't Camden also a software developer? Did they need more than one? She wasn't well-informed about software companies, but she supposed they might need more than one person with the same skills, especially if they were growing.

Molly felt her expression settle into a frustrated scowl after another conversation with a suspect in Camden's murder had revealed no real clues to his killer. She'd learned that she liked Sid Loftis, but that probably wasn't terribly useful information. The only person who hadn't been likable was Kaitlin Landry, and she could be judging the woman unfairly. After all, Kaitlin had lost her brother. It was reasonable that she'd be distressed and searching for someone to blame. And both Sid and Georgia spoke well of her.

I need to talk to Kaitlin again. But Molly couldn't see any possible way for that to happen. The woman wasn't likely to agree to a chat, no matter how friendly Sid and Georgia had found her. Plus, Kaitlin had come into Bread on Arrival, which meant no one from the bakery could go undercover to chat with her. Molly leaned back in her seat and wondered if Kaitlin had actually met everyone there. She couldn't be sure. Then she perked up. She could name one person Kaitlin definitely hadn't met. And he was charming and good with people. All she had to do was convince him to do her a tiny little favor.

As Molly mulled over her plan, she heard her name called. She glanced up to see Greer coming around the reception desk. "You wanted to talk with me?" Greer asked.

"Could we go somewhere out of earshot?" Molly's gaze flashed toward Wilma.

"Is this something I should make notes about?"

"It might be."

"Come with me." Greer led Molly through a maze of halls. They ended up in a fairly large room full of desks. Greer pulled over a chair so they could sit together at one desk. Before Molly could speak, Greer held up a finger. "First, you need to be aware that if you want to talk to Deputy Chief Gillespie after me, you'll probably have to wait for a while. He's reinterviewing all of the out-of-towners. Apparently the department is getting blowback for keeping these people here over Thanksgiving. It's putting pressure on all of us."

"I'm perfectly happy to tell you what I know," Molly said. "I had a visit from Georgia Pinter."

Greer sat up straight. "She's someone Gillespie would love to chat with. Did you learn where she's staying?"

Molly shook her head. "She didn't tell me, and she disappeared when she heard someone coming. But she said that Camden had never been her boyfriend."

Greer raised her eyebrows. "Do you believe her?"

"I think so. She acted fairly amused by the idea, but her social media page said she had a boyfriend in the software business. And Camden was a software developer. Of course, so are Nathan and Sid. I asked Sid about it a few minutes ago, and his answer was a little vague. Since he's being questioned now, you could suggest a question about Georgia be among those asked."

Greer frowned. "I can send in a note. Hold on." She got up and threaded her way through the desks while Molly waited.

Since she had a minute, Molly texted Chloe, asking her to pass on her apologies about how long she was taking. A reply came almost immediately. *Laura and Carol say not to worry about it. We got this.*

Greer returned and settled into her chair. "Okay, anything else?"

"Yes," Molly said. "Georgia said Kaitlin was in the kitchen with her when she made the tea. She told me about it as an alibi, but it also means Kaitlin had access to the tea. Plus she drives an SUV resembling the one that nearly hit Chloe. I still think the woman warrants some close attention."

"Did Georgia tell you why she was in Loch Mallaig?" Greer asked.

"No. She was very cagey about it. She also acted as if she knew nothing about the room rented in her name at Moose Lake Country Club."

"Except a woman matching her appearance was seen there," Greer said.

"Vaguely matching," Molly said. "And if it's Georgia, then she lied to me. But if so, she's a convincing liar."

Greer shrugged. "Many people are. I appreciate you coming in to share this with me. I promise to pass it all on to Gillespie, and he'll call you if he needs to talk about it further. The team is on this and taking it seriously. I think you can relax and enjoy your Thanksgiving with your daughter. Leave it in our hands."

Once again, Molly wished she could truthfully promise Greer that she would do that, but everything was too close to Chloe. Until Molly was convinced her daughter was safe, she didn't see how she could walk away. "I promise not to do anything rash."

Greer huffed. "I suppose that's the best I can hope for."

As she walked out of the police station, Molly decided to make a quick stop at The Hamper to pick up something for dinner. She hadn't stocked her refrigerator particularly well and knew the pickings would be slim without a stop for groceries.

She grabbed a basket and hurried to the produce department, planning to get a bagged salad and some deli meat and cheese. Chloe had always loved a big chef salad for supper. When she was a little girl, she'd called them "toppings salads," because of the creative ingredients they sometimes added.

As she picked up a bag of mixed greens, someone behind her called her name. Molly turned to see Fergus with a basket of his own. "What a surprise," Molly said. "I was thinking about you only a little while ago."

"Pleasant thoughts, I hope," he said.

"I was thinking how you are charming and good with people."

He raised an eyebrow. "Thank you, but why do I sense a favor brewing behind that thought?"

Molly offered a beseeching smile. "Probably because you know me well. I need someone to charm a woman who sort of hates me and everyone at the bakery."

"How did you manage to get someone to hate the whole bakery?"

"Why do you assume this is my fault?"

He laughed. "You're right. I'm sure you're perfectly innocent in this. Whom do I need to charm and why?"

Molly caught him up on everything that had happened since the Sunday meal she and Chloe had shared at his house. It took a while, and she realized that events were whirling at an amazing speed, which did nothing to make her feel better. "So now we have another attempted poisoning. Georgia Pinter is hiding out, and I think Kaitlin Landry is right in the middle of it. She is my prime suspect for nearly running over Chloe. And she made a scene at the bakehouse."

"And that's why you can't ask her questions on your own."

"Pretty much, yes," Molly said. "So are you open to doing some undercover work?"

"Sure," he said. "In fact, why don't you let me buy you some dinner, and we'll formulate a plan."

"I'd love to," Molly said. "But I need to get to work and help out, and then I'll be having supper with Chloe." She held up the basket. "Unless you want to come have chef salads with us?"

He laughed. "I enjoy salad, but I see it as something that comes with dinner, not as something you eat in place of dinner. As for the bakery, it's after closing time." He indicated the clock on the wall over the deli.

Molly yelped at the time. Sure enough, Bread on Arrival's open hours had ended. "Oh, I'm awful. I need to call in." She shifted the basket to her other arm and fished for her phone.

"Laura and Carol are familiar with how you get when you're caught up in something. I doubt they're holding it against you," Fergus said soothingly.

Molly called the bakehouse, and Carol answered cheerily, "Hey, stranger!"

"I'm sorry for being gone this long," Molly said. "I'm grabbing a salad for Chloe and me for supper, then I'll be right there."

"It's okay," Carol said. "We're actually done and cleaning up. Unless someone sneaks in an order before we can get out of here, we should be fine. And Bridget invited Chloe to dinner and a movie with some friends."

"Oh." Molly gazed down at her basket. Suddenly, buying salad fixings didn't seem so urgent. "In that case, tell Chloe I'll see her later. I'm going to get some dinner with Fergus."

"Fergus?" Carol's voice raised slightly and Molly waited for the inevitable teasing, but all Carol said was, "Send him our love and have a good time."

Molly stared down at her phone as she ended the call. *No teasing? Must be a Thanksgiving miracle.* She smiled at Fergus. "If you don't mind my running home to drop off groceries, I'd be glad to have dinner with you. Apparently I'm not needed at work, and Chloe has plans too."

Fergus returned the smile. "Their loss is my gain."

After Molly dropped off her groceries and made absolutely sure that she wasn't needed at the bakery or by her daughter, she asked Fergus if they could walk the few blocks to the Two Scots Guesthouse and deal with Kaitlin before supper. "I'm too nervous to eat anything before this is done," she said as she slipped into her coat.

"If we do that, we don't need a plotting dinner," Fergus said, reaching to help her.

"True," Molly agreed, disappointed by the realization.

Fergus grinned. "So we'll have a friends dinner instead. Right after I charm your prime suspect." He struck a pose reminiscent of an old-school general announcing the charge. "On to the guesthouse."

"They're pet-friendly. We could take Angus," Molly suggested. "He can be charming, and maybe Kaitlin is a dog person."

Fergus tilted his head slightly. "Are you afraid of this woman?"

"She could be a murderer," Molly said as she bent to snap on Angus's leash.

"But that isn't what has you worried. I'll be with you, and we're going to a public place. How abrasive was she?"

Molly stood. "Horrible. I don't much appreciate being yelled at."

"No one does, but I promise to protect you if the woman starts hurling invectives." He gestured toward Angus. "And my buddy here will bite her if she gets too rowdy."

Molly laughed but shook her head. "I hope not. I don't want to get Angus in trouble too."

Outside, the late afternoon was nearly as dark as night. It didn't help that clouds covered any hope of light from the thin moon.

Fortunately, the streets were well lit, and Molly had Fergus and Angus with her. There was no reason for the prickle of fear on the back of her neck, but she felt it anyway, as if something was warning her that danger was closer than she thought.

17

By the time they reached the guesthouse, the prickle had settled in Molly's stomach, where it lay as a knot of worry. Fergus gave her a supportive pat on the arm as he opened the door and urged her inside.

As they entered the small dining room, Myra walked out of the kitchen, drying her hands on a towel. Her face brightened as she saw Fergus and Molly. "What a nice surprise. And you brought Angus." She knelt and held out a hand to the Scottie, who recognized an invitation to be petted. He hustled over to her, tail wagging.

"I hope you don't mind about Angus," Molly said.

"Mind? He's the sweetest patron we've had today." Myra stood. "In fact, you guys are about the only patrons we've had today. Apparently nobody in town cares to take tea at a place where someone died of poisoning."

"That's terrible," Molly said. "But they're probably just busy with Thanksgiving preparations. No one could believe you or Ewan would hurt anyone." She almost winced at the end of the sentence since she had entertained the most fleeting thought of their involvement when she learned Ewan's SUV resembled the one that had nearly run over Chloe.

"I hope you're right." Myra twisted the dish towel in her hands. "And business was good before this. We were considering putting on soup for the cold months and serving that during the day. But now I'm not sure it's such a good idea."

"This will pass," Fergus said encouragingly. "The public has short memories and even shorter attention spans."

"I hope so," Myra said, then flapped her hands. "Och, listen to me talking instead of offering you two a seat. Do you want a warm drink?"

"No thank you," Molly said, though she felt bad that Myra had been expecting them to order something. "We were hoping to speak to Kaitlin Landry if she's here."

Myra shook her head. "She packed up and left right after her brother's death. Not that I blame her. I couldn't stay in the place where my brother died long before his time. Last I heard, she was over at the Moose Lake Country Club. I'm basically an empty house here."

Molly took Myra's hand. "I'll return sometime for your full tea. And I'll be sure to talk it up with our customers. In fact, one of my next marketing projects is putting up a poster in the bakery to advertise the businesses that serve our baked goods. I'll put you at the top."

"You're sweet," Myra said. "Both of you. And I suppose I should be glad of the rest with Thanksgiving tomorrow. I do have a lot to be thankful for."

"Don't we all?" Molly said, and Fergus chimed in his agreement.

When they stepped out into the night, Angus pulled them toward a patch of shadow on the guesthouse lawn he wanted to sniff.

"If we're going to the country club, we should drop Angus off at home and grab a car," Molly said as she watched her dog investigate the grounds.

"Let's take mine," Fergus suggested. "Yours has a tendency to smell like bakery, and I'm already hungry enough."

"It's barely five o'clock."

"I have a high metabolism."

"Oh, poor thing," Molly teased. "We could grab something to eat at Mulligans if you don't mind patronizing the competition."

Fergus laughed. "The country club is not my competition. Castleglen offers a totally different sort of experience. And it's good to check out other restaurants now and then. I always want Tee for Two and King's Heid Pub to be the best dining in the area."

"Having eaten at both, I can vouch for them."

Once Angus realized they were heading home again, he seemed determined to dawdle as much as possible, and Molly hated to rush him. Also, she knew she needed to hear what Kaitlin had to say, even though she wasn't eager for the confrontation.

By the time they arrived at the country club, full darkness had settled, making the drive through the wooded edge of town almost spooky. Molly was happy to relax and enjoy the ride in Fergus's Range Rover. It wasn't that she didn't love her little Honda, but the Range Rover was roomy, and the heated leather felt especially luxurious.

As they stepped out of the car, the rain that had threatened all day finally began to fall. Molly and Fergus dashed for the doors, large drops pelting them as they ran.

Inside, the lobby's warmth greeted them like a hug. Molly was grateful her coat had absorbed most of the rain. Fergus helped her slip out of it, then carried both of their jackets over to the coatrack just inside the entrance to Mulligans.

"Let's have something to eat and plan how best to confront this woman," Fergus suggested.

Since Molly didn't mind putting off the confrontation, she agreed, though she wasn't sure how much she felt like eating. They followed the hostess through the dining room, and Molly spotted something that surprised her so much she stumbled. Fergus grabbed her arm for support. As she murmured her thanks, she continued on, more slowly.

I guess it won't be hard to find Kaitlin. Directly ahead of them was a large round table with Nathan Glower, Sid Loftis, and Kaitlin Landry filling three of the five chairs.

Nathan caught sight of them as they approached. "Molly!" he called, his voice booming in the quiet room.

Molly felt as if every eye in the restaurant was focused on her, but the expressions she watched most closely were Sid's tentative smile and Kaitlin's blank stare.

"Come and join us," Nathan insisted as he rose from his seat. "And your friend too. We have plenty of room."

Although Molly knew this was the opportunity they needed, she demurred, wanting to seem polite. "We don't want to intrude."

"No intrusion," Nathan said, though Molly suspected Kaitlin would disagree. "You can help us decide what to do for Thanksgiving since we're going to be stuck here for the holiday."

Molly smiled, hoping it didn't look too forced. "I'll do my best. This is my friend Fergus MacGregor. Fergus, this is Nathan Glower."

Nathan thrust out his hand. "Nice to meet you, Fergus." He pumped Fergus's hand a couple times, then waved at Sid, who was slowly rising from his seat, and Kaitlin, who stayed seated, her stare now faintly hostile. "This is Sid Loftis and Kaitlin Landry. Fellow refugees for the holiday."

Fergus shook Sid's proffered hand, then smiled warmly at Kaitlin, who did not return the cordial expression. "I'm pleased to meet both of you."

Molly and Fergus took seats at the table, Molly carefully avoiding the chair beside Kaitlin. If she was going to try to eat something, she'd need a little distance from the open animosity radiating from that side of the table.

"I have the perfect solution to your Thanksgiving problem," Fergus said after the waitress had buzzed by to take their drink orders. "I'm hosting a Thanksgiving dinner for my employees at Castleglen. I would be delighted if you'd all enjoy the holiday meal with us as well.

I can promise the food will be excellent, since it will be prepared in the King's Heid Pub."

"That's extremely generous of you," Nathan said. "I would be honored to attend." He looked directly at Molly. "I assume you're going as well?"

"I am," Molly replied. She was more than a little surprised by Fergus's generous offer. For one, by extending his offer to the whole table, she was fairly sure he had just invited a murderer to Thanksgiving, and a murderer who poisoned people at that.

"I'll come," Sid added. "Though if the police call tonight and tell us we can go home, I'm out of here. But since that isn't likely, your offer sounds great."

With both Nathan and Sid responding, it became all the more obvious that Kaitlin was refusing to respond. Fergus positively glowed with charm as he tried to include her. "We've barely met, but I hope you'll consider having Thanksgiving with us as well. Especially since your friends will be there."

Kaitlin sniffed. "These two are not my friends. Nathan was my brother's business partner." She gestured toward Sid. "And he appears to be my brother's replacement."

"It's not that way at all," Nathan protested.

"Of course not," Kaitlin snapped. "We're all mourning my brother. Why not go to a party?" She stood up and threw her napkin on the table. "I think I'll pass on dinner tonight. I've lost my appetite." She stormed out of the restaurant.

For a moment, Molly sat frozen. Then to her own surprise, she leaped to her feet and followed Kaitlin out of the room. "Ms. Landry?" she called when they entered the lobby.

Kaitlin spun around to fix her with a withering glare. "What do you want?"

"I never had a chance to tell you that I'm sorry for the loss of your brother," Molly said. "I only spoke to him briefly, but he seemed like a kind person."

The woman stared at Molly without speaking for several seconds. Then her eyes filled, and her face softened. Her voice cracked as she said, "He was the nicest person I ever knew."

"My daughter and I would never have hurt Camden," Molly said. "Chloe said she felt they were getting to be good friends."

"I think I took some bad advice about your daughter." Kaitlin hunched her thin shoulders. "I suppose I should apologize."

"Not at all," Molly replied. "And you would be welcome at the Thanksgiving dinner. I know holidays are difficult when you're grieving. I've been there. The first holiday after the death of my husband was painful, but it was easier for me not to be alone."

Kaitlin's lips twitched. "But I am alone. Our parents died a few years ago, only days apart." She blinked rapidly. "They loved each other deeply, and I guess they couldn't be separated. Still, it left my brother and me feeling like orphans. Especially Cam. He was sensitive."

"I'm sure it helped to have you."

"I hope so. Except now I've lost him too." Kaitlin's gaze dropped to the floor. "I'm not sure about attending Thanksgiving dinner. Could you thank your friend for me? It was kind of him to offer."

"That's just how Fergus is." Molly paused, a bit frightened to disturb the delicate rapport she was building with Kaitlin. "If you see your friend Georgia, you could pass on Fergus's invitation to her as well."

Kaitlin's head snapped up. "I don't actually know Georgia all that well. I met her once at some business function with Cam and Nathan, then recognized her at the guesthouse. We chatted quite a bit, both of us being far from home. But I wouldn't call us friends, exactly."

"A business function?" Molly repeated. "Georgia is a pharmacist. Why would a tech company need a pharmacist?"

"A pharmacist?" Kaitlin echoed. "I wasn't aware that she was a pharmacist. What was she doing working in a kitchen at a bed-and-breakfast?"

"I have no idea. Didn't you wonder at the coincidence of someone you met at a business function in Milwaukee showing up as a waitress in Michigan?" Molly asked.

Kaitlin's face grew bored. "I made it a point not to pay too much attention to the business, and I couldn't remember what Georgia was doing when I saw her at that event. She could have been with catering, though I don't think she was in uniform."

"That sounds odd."

Kaitlin raised one shoulder in a weak shrug. "Blocking out the business was a defense mechanism. Cam would talk me to death about apps and programs if I showed the slightest interest. My brother was a sweetheart, but he never understood that not everyone is fascinated by computer coding."

"Should I ask Nathan?" Molly asked.

"He would know. The company sometimes hired consultants when working on building an app. If Georgia was a pharmacist, they could have been working on something for a pharmaceutical company. Nathan was always pushing Cam to create more basic service apps. It could have been something as simple as an app to help people keep track of their meds. Again, your best bet is to ask Nathan."

"I thought someone told me you were employed at the company."

Kaitlin laughed. "I was on the payroll, but it was basically a way for Cam to help out with my bills. I didn't work there. I'd come in to schmooze when they had big money clients or at social events since neither Nathan nor Cam were married. Nathan said some deals work better if we acted like a family company. Anyway, I was paid to be social."

"How was the company doing?" Molly asked. She assumed it was thriving since they were apparently luring Sid in to work for them.

"I didn't handle the books, but I couldn't talk about it even if I did. There's one thing Nathan says over and over. Rumors about a company's finances can be deadly." Kaitlin exhaled sharply. "Now if you'll excuse me, I think I've had enough socializing for one evening."

Molly felt no urge to continue the conversation as she watched Kaitlin walk away. With her almost emotionless delivery, Kaitlin's last words had left Molly with a chill.

When Molly returned to the table, Nathan was lifting his glass in a toast. "To my dear friend Cam," he said. "I miss him."

As Nathan sipped his drink, Molly took her seat beside Fergus. "It must be hard. I can tell Kaitlin is suffering too."

Nathan nodded solemnly. "Cam was my friend as well as my business partner. He could be a handful, but I keep thinking of things I want to text him about. I guess you don't realize how much a person means to you until they're gone."

Fresh from her conversation with Kaitlin, Molly wanted to ask Nathan about Georgia's work for the company, but she felt it would be insensitive to pull attention to the investigation. She decided to wait. Perhaps it would fit in better over dinner.

Unfortunately, she never found an opportunity to work in talk of Kaitlin or Georgia. Nathan seemed determined to drive the dinner conversation, and he peppered Fergus with questions about Loch Mallaig. "I'm eager to meet more new people tomorrow," he explained. "I want to be able to talk to them about their hometown."

Sid spoke in a gloomy tone. "It's not that I don't enjoy new people, but I sure wish I was home with all my old people."

Molly tried for a teasing grin. "Your sister may not appreciate being called 'old people.'"

At that Sid actually smiled. "I call her old all the time. She was born three whole minutes before me."

Though the dinner was far more pleasant than Molly had expected, she still felt frustrated. She'd talked to Kaitlin and even gained some ground in smoothing the woman's ruffled feathers, but she hadn't learned much—although now she did wonder about Georgia's relationship to Nathan's company. Molly made a mental note to ask Nathan directly about it over Thanksgiving, even if she had to wedge it into conversation.

When dinner was over, Molly and Fergus said their goodbyes and walked out into the night. The rain had stopped, but the cold, moist air was bracing.

Molly shivered, then looked sideways at Fergus. "I assume you're aware that you may have invited a killer to Thanksgiving. Specifically one who favors poisoning."

"The way I see it, if there is someone dangerous lurking in Loch Mallaig, I want to keep the person where I can watch him or her." Fergus opened the car door for Molly. "That's the best way I can think of to keep my real friends safe."

"It should make for an interesting party," Molly replied as she slipped inside. While Fergus walked around the Range Rover to get to the driver's side door, she added under her breath, "As long as it doesn't get too interesting." But she had a bad feeling that it might.

18

When Molly got home from dinner with Fergus, she settled down on the sofa, determined to finish the book she'd borrowed from the library. Despite the uneasiness caused by the plot's spooky twists and turns, she was soon lost in the swirling fog of the moors and the dangers that lurked in the dark. Angus joined her on the sofa, and Molly was glad of his warm, comforting presence as the story's main character found herself in deeper and deeper peril.

Molly had just decided it was the bad-tempered housekeeper who was trying to drive the poor main character insane when the young heroine stumbled across a body lying on the stone floor of the kitchen. She knelt and held her candle close to identify the unfortunate victim. The main character discovered with a gasp that it was the housekeeper. Molly echoed the heroine's gasp, albeit more softly. *If it's not the housekeeper, who is it?*

Frustrated, she set the book in her lap and glanced over at the clock. It was getting late, at least for someone keeping baker's hours. Molly stretched, enjoying the fact that she didn't need to set her alarm clock. The bakery was closed until Monday. She could sleep in for so many days, she'd forget what it was like to shuffle around in the dark, searching for her slippers. Normally Thanksgiving would have her up early as well, but since she and Chloe would be eating at Castleglen, she didn't even have to prepare any food.

"I'm going to enjoy being a woman of leisure," Molly told Angus, who merely opened one eye before slipping off to sleep. *Or at least I would enjoy being a woman of leisure if Camden Landry's murder was solved.* She wasn't sure sharing Thanksgiving with a bunch of murder suspects was the best idea either.

Molly peered at the clock again and wondered when Chloe would be home. She was glad Bridget had included her in an outing. Chloe needed to have some fun, and though Bridget was considerably younger than Molly's daughter, she was definitely fun. She'd rarely seen Bridget when she wasn't in good spirits.

Molly considered her book again, but without enthusiasm. She could give up and go to bed, but she wasn't sure she could sleep with Chloe out. Molly chuckled at that notion. Chloe was twenty-seven, and Molly doubted she'd ever get over waiting up for her. "Though these are special circumstances," she said aloud. Angus didn't even bother to open an eye this time, so Molly yawned, stretched, and went back to debating whether she should go to bed.

Before she could come to a decision, she heard the lock turning in the outside door that led into the office. She got up, causing Angus to grumble, and went to greet Chloe.

Chloe held up a key. "Carol gave this to me so I wouldn't have to wake you. Sorry I did anyway."

"I wasn't sleeping," Molly replied. "I was scaring myself silly with the book Grizela forced on me. How was your evening?"

Chloe flipped the lock, then beamed at her. "Fun. Bridget and her friends are hilarious. I almost felt like I was back in college."

"I'm glad you had such a nice time," Molly said as they walked to the den.

"You should have heard Bridget's stories about her extended family at Thanksgiving." Chloe giggled. "Apparently she has an uncle who is quite a character."

They settled on the sofa, on either side of a sleepy dog. Chloe shared some of Bridget's stories, and they laughed together. Then Molly caught sight of the time again. "I should head off to bed. My head is starting to feel a little woolly."

"I think I'll spend a little time winding down." Chloe picked up the book Molly had set aside. "Besides, I haven't quite finished this."

Molly wrinkled her nose at it. "I found out I had guessed the wrong culprit, so the book is both scary and frustrating."

"You thought it was the housekeeper, right?" Chloe asked. "Me too. I won't tell you who I think it is now. I don't want to spoil it, but I suspect you have to apply a little Sherlock Holmes."

"Sherlock Holmes?"

Chloe sat up straight and peered down her nose at her mother, putting on a truly awful British accent. "Once you eliminate the impossible, whatever remains, no matter how improbable, must be the truth."

"I'll keep that in mind," Molly said. She gave her daughter a kiss on the cheek and headed off to bed. She wondered if that advice would help her figure out who had killed Camden. But all the suspects were possible, right? And all equally unlikely.

Molly climbed into bed and snapped off the light. "Thanks for nothing, Sherlock."

On Thanksgiving morning, the sunbeams coming through the bedroom window seemed determined to make up for the gloom of the night before. The sunshine was so cheering that Molly was humming under her breath by the time she got to the kitchen, lured there by the smell of coffee. Chloe sat at the table, gazing out at the beautiful morning.

"Good morning." Molly stopped to pour coffee. "What a gorgeous day."

Chloe nodded. "It does make it easier to think about things I'm thankful for. Speaking of which, I'm thankful we wear the same size because I need to borrow a dress. I didn't come home expecting to attend a fancy dinner party."

"You're welcome to anything I own," Molly assured her, "but I don't think Fergus intends this to be overly fancy. He wants it to be homey."

"Homey if you live in a mansion," Chloe said. "How about semi-fancy?"

"That's about all my wardrobe offers anyway." Molly carried her coffee to the table and settled across from Chloe. "And speaking of the dinner, I have news you probably won't be happy about."

Chloe regarded her mother over the edge of the coffee cup. She didn't speak, though she did raise her eyebrows in question.

"Last night, Fergus invited the rest of the Milwaukee people to dinner today," Molly said.

Chloe set her mug on the table with a *thump*. "Why?"

"His motives were a bit mixed, but I think he honestly felt bad about them being far from home for such a family-oriented holiday. Sid Loftis is miserable. His family must be close."

Chloe sat back in her chair. "That's nice, I guess. But I don't want Kaitlin Landry shrieking another murder accusation at me. I'm sorry that she's hurting, but that's not how I want to spend my Thanksgiving. And it's not the first thing I want to remember when I think of Camden."

"Actually, I talked to Kaitlin last night," Molly said. "I think she's mellowing. At the very least, I don't expect any shouting. Though it's probably best if you keep your distance from her if she's there."

"I'm all for that." Chloe got up. "I'm going to go raid your closet.

I may need to try on some things, and I want an early start. Once I pick the outfit, I can think about what to do with my hair."

As Molly watched her daughter leave, she wondered if she should put more thought into her own clothes. She'd been planning something simple. She took a long swallow of her coffee and spoke firmly. "I'm a simple woman, and I'll go with that."

After her cup was empty, she decided to take Angus for a walk to work up an appetite for breakfast. As she shrugged into her coat, she called out to Chloe that she was leaving, then snapped a leash on Angus and headed out. The quick change from the warmth of the apartment to the chilly morning breeze was startling and Molly slipped gloves from her coat pockets to put on.

If Angus was bothered by the cold air, he showed no sign of it. Instead he trotted out of the fenced area at a jaunty pace, only putting his nose down to begin his investigative sniffing after they were through the gate.

The grass crunched slightly under Molly's feet as they passed under a tree, the shade having kept the frost from melting. "How about a walk around Dumfries Park?" she suggested.

As if he understood, Angus barked in happy agreement.

The park stretched along the downtown section of Yooper Boulevard, close enough to the banks of Loch Mallaig that Molly could see the boats tied up at the pier. Not surprisingly, she didn't see anyone out on the loch. In the summer, she had seen sailboats and kayaks every day, but the chill of autumn was even colder over the water.

Angus stopped suddenly, staring toward the cinder-block building where the town stored equipment and supplies for the park. He barked once, the sound as sharp as the cold, then pulled against the leash, clearly eager to reach the building. Molly squinted dubiously in that direction. She knew there were trash cans over there and wondered if Angus was smelling a raccoon. It was early enough in the morning that a four-legged bandit might not have finished raiding the trash yet.

"We should leave whatever it is alone," she told the little dog. But Angus was relentless, hauling on the leash so hard Molly worried that he would choke himself.

Giving in at last, she scooped him up. "Fine, we'll walk over there. But I'm not putting you down to fight with a skunk or a raccoon." Though he didn't squirm in her arms, Angus stayed focused on the building.

She'd nearly reached the edge of the cement pad around the shed when Angus began barking. Molly stopped, suddenly aware of how alone she was in the frozen park. That's when someone stepped around a shadowy corner of the building. "Molly Ferris?"

Molly recognized the voice before she could identify the heavily bundled figure. "Georgia?"

Georgia walked over, and Angus stopped barking. Instead he wagged his tail, and Georgia smiled a little at him. "He's sure a cute little fella," she said. She reached out to pat Angus and got her fingers licked in the bargain.

"What are you doing in the park?" Molly asked.

Georgia's expression was hard to read. "I followed you. I wanted to speak to you, but I had to be sure no one would see us."

"Because the police are hunting for you."

Georgia waved that away. "I'm not worried about the police." She paused, then added, "Not much anyway. I didn't kill anyone, even though everyone thinks I did. I know I haven't convinced you yet either, but I will."

"It doesn't matter what I think. You should go to the police station and explain yourself," Molly insisted. "The Loch Mallaig police aren't in the habit of railroading innocent people."

"I will, the minute I find the proof I need. I'm close." She paused, appearing to struggle with a decision. Finally she said, "I know who killed Camden. It's the last person I ever expected, but I'm sure. I just need to get the evidence to prove it. Otherwise it's only my word, and I'm not certain I have much credibility in Loch Mallaig. Thanks in part to you."

"Who is it?" Molly asked.

Georgia surveyed the park. "I'm not sure I should tell you. It could put you in danger."

"Georgia, if you're afraid, why are you in Loch Mallaig?" Molly asked.

"Because what happens when I go home and no one cares about what happened here? And the murderer has all the time in the world to kill me?"

"You should tell me," Molly said. "I can pass on your theory to the police. At the very least, it will give them a direction to investigate."

Georgia shook her head, her black hair swinging into her face like ribbons of darkness. "We can't tip off the killer."

"Why?"

The sound of tires on gravel reached them, eliciting a yelp from Georgia. Someone on Yooper Boulevard was pulling off the road and into the smallest of the parking areas for the long park. Molly stood frozen, gripping Angus as her gaze stayed locked on the car. The passenger side door opened and Molly almost whimpered with relief. She recognized the man who stepped out as a local who wasn't even remotely connected with the crazy events of the last few days. He unloaded a Labrador retriever from the back seat, and Molly realized the man had come to the park for the same reason as she and Angus.

She turned back to reassure Georgia, but the woman was gone. "Georgia?" Molly called. "It's okay. I know that man." She didn't actually remember his name, but he went to her church. "Georgia?"

There was no answer from the area around the storage building. Georgia Pinter was gone. Again.

Molly set Angus on the ground. "Can you find Georgia?" she asked. "Where did she go?" Since Georgia had petted Angus a little while she'd talked to Molly, there was every chance Angus would go searching for his new friend.

Unfortunately the Labrador from the car proved too much of a distraction, and Angus did his best to haul Molly across the park for a meeting. With a sigh, Molly let him say hello.

Even while she exchanged pleasantries with the dog's owner, Molly's head was swirling with questions. Who could Georgia have been talking about? Who would everyone least suspect of the murder? Was Georgia truly as afraid as she appeared, or was she only using Molly, hoping to deflect suspicion away from herself by convincing Molly she was innocent with these ridiculous clandestine meetings?

With no answers and plenty of frustration, Molly and Angus said goodbye to their new friends and headed for home.

19

When Molly and Angus got to the apartment, Chloe trotted out of the bedroom and stopped to do a spin. "What do you think?" she asked. "Was this a good choice?"

Chloe wore a long-sleeved sweater dress that featured a scalloped-edge neckline dotted with small embroidered flowers. The blue knit fabric was super soft, and the dress skimmed Chloe's curves without being too tight anywhere. Molly had originally bought the dress because the shade of blue exactly matched her eyes. Chloe's eyes were brown, like her father's, but the blue set off her fair skin and blonde hair well.

"I think it's perfect," Molly said. "And I'll try not to be grumpy that it looks better on you."

"You weren't planning to wear it, were you?" Chloe asked, suddenly concerned. "I could pick something different."

"No, that's fine. I bought a new sweater and skirt that I haven't worn yet. It's cozy too. After my walk in the park, I think this is definitely a day for warm clothes." Molly considered telling Chloe about her meeting with Georgia, but she was hesitant to do anything to dim the happiness on Chloe's face. They were having Thanksgiving together. That was practically a little miracle right there, and Molly didn't want to dampen its joy.

"Oh," Chloe said, cutting into Molly's thoughts, "Fergus called. He said one of his employees is bringing her son's dog. Apparently she's dog sitting, and the dog can't be left alone with the woman's cat.

Fergus said that since he's throwing the door open for one dog, he wanted to invite Angus as well."

"Hmm." Molly eyed Angus, who was flopped on a nearby rug, snuggling up to Woolie. "I don't want to have to worry about Angus's behavior. What if he begs and annoys the other guests?"

"Aw, Mom, please?" For an instant, Chloe resembled the little girl she had once been, eager to talk Molly into some new creature she wanted to bring into the house. "I'm not going to know a lot of the people, and Angus is a great icebreaker. I'll watch him."

Molly hated to deny Chloe when she'd been through some rough days. And the party would be in a conference room, which meant she didn't have to worry about Angus upsetting any of Castleglen's paying guests. The staff dinner would be full of people who mostly already knew Angus.

"Okay, honey. You win."

"In that case, I'm going to find a scarf or something for Angus to wear," Chloe said. "Wouldn't he be gorgeous in a nice red plaid bow tie? Oh, I wish I'd thought ahead. I could have bought him one when I was shopping."

"Actually, he owns one," Molly said. "But I won't promise he'll be willing to wear it long. You should wait until we get to Castleglen to put it on him. That way, a few people will see it before he figures out how to get out of it."

"Do you want me to help you hunt for it?" Chloe asked.

Molly laughed. "What makes you think I don't know exactly where it is?"

"Do you?" Chloe said innocently.

"I don't need help finding it," Molly told her, which wasn't quite an answer, but it was the only one Molly planned to give her.

"No problem." Chloe chuckled as she headed to the sofa. "I only have a few pages left of this book."

Molly headed into her bedroom and began going through her catchall on the dresser, trying to remember where she had tossed the bow tie after learning Angus wasn't overly thrilled about costuming. She'd just found it when her phone rang, and she grabbed it. To her delight, the call was from her mom.

Molly's parents, Janet and Daniel Kirkpatrick, lived in Davenport, Iowa, which meant that Molly didn't see them as much as she wished. Her parents knew Loch Mallaig well, though, as they'd visited every summer during most of Molly's childhood.

"I haven't caught you in the middle of baking or stuffing a turkey, have I?" Janet asked in lieu of a greeting.

"No, I'm stuffing free today," Molly said as she sank down on the edge of the bed. "Chloe and I are going to have Thanksgiving at Castleglen. Fergus invited us."

"Chloe is home?" Surprise colored Janet's voice.

"I think Chloe considers Milwaukee home," Molly said with barely a wince. "But she is here with me. The vet clinic had an infestation of bats and they're closed over the holiday to remove them. The bats' loss is my gain."

"Is she around?" her mom asked. "I'll want to say hi before I hang up."

Molly twirled the bow tie absently in her fingers. "Of course. How is your Thanksgiving going? Are Graham and his family coming to dinner?" Molly felt a wistful pang. It had been a while since she'd seen her brother, his wife, Libby, or their son, Jamey, who was a couple years younger than Chloe.

"Graham and Libby are," her mom said cheerfully. "But Jamey has a new girlfriend and is having Thanksgiving with her family. Libby is none too pleased about that. It's tough when your kids don't have holidays at home anymore." Her mom's sigh was so deep and dramatic that Molly almost laughed. She felt the message behind it, and she could agree with the sentiment. It was tough having holidays without Chloe too.

"Everyone could move to Loch Mallaig," Molly said. "It's lovely here, and we'd have all our holidays together."

Janet laughed. "I could sell that one to your father. He adores Loch Mallaig. But I'm sure Graham and Libby wouldn't move, so I guess we'll stay here for now."

"You're not overdoing it with the Thanksgiving prep, are you?" Molly asked. Janet had lupus, though she managed the disease well. Still, she sometimes pushed her body harder than she should, especially considering she was seventy-eight years old.

"I'm fine," Janet said. "Libby is bringing all the side dishes. I'm strictly turkey and dessert this year. Which reminds me, I'm going to have to check on it in a few. Can I chat with Chloe a little before I go?"

"Of course." Molly hopped off the bed and carried her phone to Chloe. "Your grandmother wants to talk to you."

Chloe squealed and tossed the book down beside her. "Gram!" she gushed into the phone the second Molly handed it to her.

Molly dropped the bow tie into Chloe's lap, then headed into the kitchen for another cup of coffee. She settled down at the table near the window and gazed out at the autumn day. She was glad to be in Loch Mallaig, but she did miss time with her mom and dad.

"It's not as if I'm a million miles away," she said aloud. "I could drive down to see them." Her window of opportunity for doing that before weather shut everyone in was rapidly closing, however. Molly had no interest in a snowy road trip. And then there was the bakehouse, which needed all hands on deck through the holiday season—not that she'd been abiding by that the way she should have been lately.

Angus wandered into the kitchen and sat at her feet, peering up at her curiously. "Yes," she told him. "I am talking to myself." Angus's stubby tail wagged, and Molly reached down to run her fingers through his wiry coat. "Fergus has invited you to Thanksgiving," she told him. "I hope you'll be on your best behavior."

Angus sat up on his back legs and pawed the air, one of his more endearing tricks, which he tended to reserve for when he smelled food.

"No snacks," she told him. "I expect you'll finagle plenty of goodies out of people at Castleglen."

Since no treat had appeared, Angus flopped down at Molly's feet.

Chloe walked into the room with the phone in her hand. "Gram wants to talk to you again," Chloe said and mouthed, "You're in trouble."

Molly took the phone. "Mom?"

"Why didn't you tell me that a friend of Chloe's was killed? You're staying strictly out of it, I hope. That insatiable curiosity of yours gets you in trouble."

Molly gaped at Chloe in surprise as her daughter poured herself a mug of coffee. Molly wouldn't have expected Chloe to bring up the murder, but then, Chloe and her grandmother had always been close. "We're strictly focused on Thanksgiving here," Molly assured her mother, hoping she'd be forgiven the fib, since it was in the interest of preserving Janet's enjoyment of her holiday.

Janet harrumphed. "I hope so. Chloe deserves a nice Thanksgiving. She's clearly been through a lot."

Chloe slipped into the seat across from Molly and mouthed, "Sorry."

Molly offered her mom several more assurances, but it was the distant sound of a doorbell that made Janet stop scolding her.

"Libby and Graham are here. I have to run," she said. "You two have a nice, *safe* Thanksgiving."

"We will, Mom. I promise." Molly disconnected the call and raised an eyebrow at Chloe.

"I didn't mean to rat you out and put Gram in a state," Chloe said. "I had Camden's death on my mind and it came out of my mouth."

"Do you want to talk about it?" Molly asked.

"Not really."

Silence fell between them, and they both stared out the window. Though nearly all the trees in sight were bare, the view of Loch Mallaig never failed to captivate. Molly even saw a boat on the lake. Some hearty soul was braving the cold.

Chloe sighed. "It is lovely here. The kitchen window at my place in Milwaukee looks out on a sad walled garden and an alley. You'd have to love bricks to consider it attractive."

"You can always come here for a dose of beautiful views," Molly promised. "Loch Mallaig doesn't lack them." She glanced at the time on her phone. "I should go get dressed. We'll need to leave fairly soon."

Molly headed to her room to change. She was feeling a little melancholy, but if she knew Fergus, his Thanksgiving celebration would clear that up. He was a wonderful host.

She slipped into the new skirt and sweater and approved of what she saw in the mirror. Though the dusty-rose hue didn't bring out her eyes the way the dress Chloe had chosen did, the color did brighten Molly's fair complexion.

"It'll do," she said softly to her mirror, then gave herself a chagrined smile. She'd have to watch the talking to herself. Wasn't that a bad sign?

When Molly and Chloe arrived at Castleglen, they found the parking lot surprisingly full. Apparently the resort wasn't experiencing the same lack of guests befalling Moose Lake Country Club and Two Scots Guesthouse.

"I guess Castleglen is the place to be for Thanksgiving," Chloe observed as her mother drove slowly through the lot, searching for a parking space.

"I wonder if I should have tried the staff lot," Molly said. "Though if all the staff is here too, it probably isn't any better."

They finally found a spot, but it would be a bit of a hike to the side entrance that led most directly to the large conference room where the staff dinner would be served.

"On the bright side," Molly said as she shut off the engine, "Angus will have a nice walk before we get into the building."

"Always good to see the silver lining," Chloe said.

Molly opened her door carefully since one of the cars next to hers had parked over the line, leaving her limited space to get in and out of the car. She squeezed out, careful not to let her wool dress coat brush against the side of the car.

She met Chloe behind the Fit, where Chloe handed her Angus. "Hold on to him a second, please. I'll put on his bow tie."

"Good luck," Molly said. But to her shock, Angus was perfectly content to have the plaid bow tie snapped around his neck. He didn't wriggle a bit, and when Chloe set him on the pavement, he didn't try to paw at the bow.

"I don't know why you assumed he wouldn't wear it," Chloe said.

"I'm beginning to think your power over my dog is scary," Molly told her.

"I promise to use my power only for good," Chloe said solemnly as they walked across the crowded parking lot to reach the sidewalk tucked behind tall bushes. The sidewalk was easy to access, but by not drawing too much attention to it, visitors would be more inclined to use the front entrance of the main lodge, which was the resort's preference. The front entrance put visitors close to the restaurants, the spa, and the gift shop.

Molly appreciated the warmth of her long coat. The breeze was chilly on her ankles. "Are you warm enough?" she asked her daughter.

"Not warm enough to loiter," Chloe said. "But I'll be fine for going in and out."

They circled around the large bushes and stepped onto the narrow sidewalk. Instead of heading toward the building, however, Angus pulled hard on the leash, clearly wanting to explore the shrubbery.

"No," Chloe said firmly. "Not now, Angus."

For once, Chloe's impressive connection with Angus didn't help at all. The little dog didn't respond to her tugging on the leash or her words.

"Maybe I'd better carry him," Molly said as she stepped closer.

To her shock, Angus twisted and pulled hard, causing his collar to slip over his head, taking the bow tie with it. In an instant, Chloe was holding a dangling leash and Molly was bending over to snatch at air. Angus dashed into the bushes.

Molly moaned. Angus never misbehaved this much. "Angus, come here!"

Chloe knelt near the edge of the bushes. "Angus?" she peered into the thick bush. "Something is in there."

"Angus, come!" Molly commanded in alarm, suddenly worried that whatever was in the bushes would hurt the little dog.

To their surprise, Angus emerged a moment later, tail first, dragging something behind him. In an instant, Molly saw it was the sleeve of a hoodie. And someone was wearing it. Someone very, very still.

Once Angus had gotten their attention, he let go of the arm. Chloe crawled into the bush to reach the person. "Mom, it's Georgia."

"Is she alive?" Molly asked. She knelt to touch the woman's hand. It was ice-cold.

20

Molly wasn't sure she'd ever feel warm again as she stood clutching Angus inside the Castleglen conference room. Chloe stood beside her, her face a picture of worry. Molly took her daughter's hand. "You did all you could. Those stab wounds looked pretty serious."

"I hope what I did was enough," Chloe whispered. When the ambulance had arrived, Georgia was unconscious but alive. Molly was sure that was due to her daughter's efforts.

When the ambulance finally loaded Georgia and left, Chloe had gone straight to a restroom to wash blood from her hands and dab at the smears of dirt and leaves on the blue dress. She'd nearly cried when she came out, clearly having failed to clean the stains. It had taken Molly several minutes to convince her daughter that the dress didn't matter.

"Regardless of the outcome, you were wonderful," Molly insisted. "I'm proud of you."

Chloe managed a weak smile.

Molly's gaze swept the conference room. The Castleglen staff stood in small groups around the room, speaking quietly. Some nibbled appetizers, though the thought of eating anything knotted Molly's stomach. She saw Fergus speaking quietly to the Milwaukee group, who all appeared shocked and saddened.

Deputy Chief Gillespie stepped into the room through one of the two doors that led to the large conference room. He scanned the room, then approached Molly and Chloe. "You've been at a lot of crime scenes lately, Molly."

"And I'll be happy to stop," Molly replied, trying to mimic the light tone the deputy chief had used, but suspecting she hadn't quite nailed it.

"Will you keep us updated on Georgia's condition?" Chloe asked. "I need to know."

"Of course," Gillespie said. "The ambulance drivers said that Georgia will owe her life to your efforts. That and the cold slowing her blood loss."

"I hope it's enough." Chloe rubbed her own arms, apparently feeling a chill.

"I'm sorry that you've both been through a difficult time, but I have questions," the deputy chief went on.

"Absolutely," Chloe agreed. "Whatever we can do to help."

"I want to go through what happened," Gillespie said, "including how you spotted the body."

"I doubt we would have seen anything." Molly shifted Angus in her arms, giving him another hug. "Georgia was completely under the bush. Angus must have known she was there. He rushed under and was trying to pull her out, which is how we saw her at all. I couldn't tell who it was until Chloe crawled under the bush and identified her. I should have recognized the hoodie, but I was so shocked."

"And you'd both arrived at Castleglen only minutes before?" Gillespie asked.

Molly bobbed her head. "We had to drive around a little to find parking, but Angus alerted us to the bushes as we were walking to the door."

"That's not the usual way to come into the lodge."

"No." Molly must have been hugging Angus too tightly because the little dog began to wiggle.

"Here, Mom," Chloe said, holding out her hands. "Let me hold him."

Molly reluctantly handed over the little terrier. She instantly felt colder and shivered.

Chloe picked up the recitation. "Mom knew the shortest path to the conference room."

The deputy chief's expression was unreadable. "Prior to finding her, when was the last time you saw Georgia?"

"A few hours ago," Molly said. "She approached me at Dumfries Park when I was walking Angus. She said she knew who had killed Camden, and that it was the last person she'd suspected."

"But she didn't say who?"

Molly shook her head. "I asked, but Georgia was scared away by a car pulling into the lot at the park, even though it was just another dog owner. Georgia was jumpy the whole time. She seemed scared. I told her to go to the police, but she thought she'd be arrested and the killer would go free."

The deputy chief frowned. "We don't operate that way."

"Of course not," Molly said. "And I said as much to Georgia, but I couldn't convince her." Molly's voice grew rough as she added, "I should have tried harder."

"No, Mom," Chloe said. "You can't think that. You did your best."

Molly gave her daughter a grateful hug around her armful of Angus. "So did you." Then she turned to the deputy chief. "I do wonder about the comings and goings of the rest of the folks from Milwaukee. If Georgia knew her attacker, if she was right about her suspicions, it was one of them."

The deputy chief smiled ruefully. "I will be talking to each of them, but I want you to stay out of it." He surveyed the room. "In fact, what are all our suspects doing at Thanksgiving dinner for the Castleglen staff?"

"I invited them." Fergus stepped into the group and handed

Molly a mug. "Hot chocolate. I could see you shivering across the room." He offered a second mug to Chloe. "I have one for you too. It's okay to put Angus down. You can even let him off the leash if you want."

Chloe carefully put Angus on the floor and unsnapped his leash, as if reluctant to let go of him after their latest close call. Instead of wandering off to explore, Angus sat between Chloe and Molly. Chloe stood and took the mug from Fergus, murmuring her thanks.

"Fergus, why did you invite a group of strangers to Thanksgiving?" Gillespie asked.

"They were far from home and fairly miserable," Fergus said. "I felt bad for them. Also, I was worried about Molly and Chloe, and thought it would be safer if we knew where everyone was. I may have been mistaken about that."

"Can you tell me when each of them got here?" Gillespie asked.

"They arrived separately," Fergus said. "I remember thinking that was weird. They're all staying at the Moose Lake Country Club, so it would have made more sense to drive over together."

"Who arrived first?"

"Kaitlin Landry. And, for the record, she was completely unflustered and not acting as if she attacked someone outside."

"And what time exactly did she arrive?"

"That I can't tell you," Fergus said. "I was in and out as I made sure everything was running smoothly. She was simply here when I came in once. She was shrugging out of her coat, and I assumed she'd just arrived. Kaitlin had a beverage by the time Sid Loftis came in. He didn't appear particularly murderous either. He went straight over to chat with Kaitlin."

"Which means Nathan Glower came in last," the deputy chief said.

"Yes, but he didn't seem any more distressed than the others," Fergus replied. "I find it hard to believe that someone could attack a woman and leave her for dead, then walk casually into a social gathering."

Gillespie shrugged. "I never bet against what people are capable of." He shifted his gaze from Fergus to Molly to Chloe. "I can't make you cancel this event, but I caution all of you to be careful. Once I speak with those three, I'll need to leave." He paused and refocused on Fergus. "I could question all of your staff, but I want to get home to my own Thanksgiving. Could you ask around and find out if anyone saw anything out of the ordinary?"

"I thought you wanted us to stay out of it," Chloe said, surprising Molly with the sharpness of her tone.

"I want you and your mother to stay out of it," the chief replied. "You've been in the middle of too much, and I'm worried about you both. I'm only asking Fergus to help because his staff will be more inclined to tell him small details that they thought were unimportant. I don't appreciate seeing any of you socializing with our prime suspects, but I can't do much about it." He straightened up, a signal that he was done chatting. "Thank you for answering my questions."

Gillespie headed for the small group from Milwaukee. Angus left his post beside Chloe and Molly to trot over to Fergus and sniff his shoes.

Fergus put a hand on Molly's arm. "Are you all right?" He glanced toward Chloe. "Both of you?"

"No," Chloe answered before Molly could. "This is crazy. Georgia could die. Camden did die. Nathan Glower was hospitalized. What's going on? I thought I'd be coming here for a few peaceful days with my mom in a quiet little town."

Molly shared her daughter's frustration. "I wish I knew what was going on. I think Georgia was attacked for what she had figured out. She must have confronted the killer."

"But she was hiding from the killer," Chloe said. "Wasn't she?"

Molly nodded. "And from the police, until she figured out who had killed Camden and could prove it. Maybe once she had done that, she believed that person wouldn't hurt her for some reason."

"Aren't you two doing exactly what the deputy chief told you not to do?" Fergus asked.

"We're not interfering," Molly said. "We're discussing. Since I'm fairly sure you're not the killer, Fergus, we should be safe."

Fergus put his hand to his chest. "Fairly? Thanks for the vote of confidence."

"This isn't funny," Chloe snapped. "None of this is funny. If the police department here is so great, why did I have to crawl under a bush to try to save someone's life?"

Angus yipped at the angry tone in her voice and took up a position exactly in the middle of the three of them, his head turning as each person spoke, giving him the appearance of a spectator at a tennis match.

"Because no police department is magic," Molly said, trying to calm her daughter. "We're not taking the attack on Georgia lightly, but we shouldn't let it make us forget that there are things to be thankful for. One of those things is you. Another is Angus. If he hadn't alerted us to Georgia's body, we would have missed her. And thanks to your medical training, she now has a chance to survive."

Chloe pressed her lips together, then relaxed her shoulders. "You're right, Mom. I shouldn't be so hard on them. I'm sure they're doing all they can. I just want this to be over."

"We all do. And it will be soon," Molly said, squeezing her hand and hoping her words were true.

"Why would someone leave her under a bush that every guest at Thanksgiving would have to pass?" Fergus asked. "Especially considering Georgia was still alive. What if she had crawled out and gotten help?"

"I keep thinking about that," Chloe said as she studied the small group surrounding the deputy chief. "There's no way Kaitlin could have dragged Georgia under that bush, even if Georgia was too weak to struggle much. Deadweight is hard to move. I can say that from experience, having carried my share of large, unconscious dogs."

"That leaves Nathan or Sid," Molly said.

Chloe shook her head. "None of them could have dragged someone under a bush. Look at me." She gestured toward the stained dress. "If one of them is the killer, how did he clean up perfectly?"

"If he wore a long coat, taking it off would remove much of the evidence," Fergus suggested.

"Not on the knees of their pants," Chloe insisted.

Molly pondered that. "What if none of them dragged Georgia under the bush?"

Chloe groaned. "You think there are more suspects?"

"No," Molly said. "What if someone attacked Georgia, but she got away? And what if she hid from the killer under the bush in an area where she knew people would be coming and going?"

"That doesn't make sense." Fergus furrowed his brow. "She surely would have come inside where someone could help her."

"Not if the killer was between her and the way inside," Molly said, then added, "Georgia said the killer was the one she least expected."

"Who would that be?" Fergus asked.

"According to Myra, Georgia and Kaitlin were chummy," Molly said. "If Kaitlin was her friend, she might have believed she wouldn't hurt her."

"But Kaitlin said she barely knew her," Fergus replied.

"Which is exactly what she would say if she was trying to deflect attention," Chloe said. "Plus, in all the murder mysteries, they always say that poison is a woman's weapon."

"Except that Georgia wasn't poisoned," Molly reminded her.

Chloe shuddered. "No, she wasn't. But she could have surprised Kaitlin, who had to make use of whatever was at hand." She waved toward the appetizer table. "I don't suppose you're missing a knife over there, Fergus?"

"The kitchen is doing a count," Fergus said. "It was one of the first questions the police asked. But if it is one of our knives, any of them could have picked it up."

"But only if the person went outside afterward," Molly said. "Did any of them leave the room?"

"More specifically, did Kaitlin leave the room?" Chloe asked. "She's the most probable suspect. You said she inherits everything from Camden."

"That's what Nathan told me," Molly said.

"Nathan, who was poisoned," Chloe added. "Which means he's not our killer. And you said Sid isn't likely."

"He's mostly sad to be away from home," Molly agreed. "That doesn't exclude him, though."

"Except he doesn't have a motive." Chloe turned to Fergus. "Did he leave the room after he arrived?"

"Not that I saw," Fergus answered. "But I was in and out. I can't say with certainty that any of the three didn't leave. I wish I'd paid more attention, but I didn't expect an attempted murder."

"Doesn't matter," Chloe said firmly. "The killer is Kaitlin Landry."

Molly contemplated her daughter's determined expression. She wasn't at all sure that Kaitlin was the killer, though she had to admit that Chloe's logic was impeccable, even if they ignored the fact that Chloe had nearly been run over by an SUV exactly like the one Kaitlin drove.

Molly shifted her attention to where the deputy chief was interviewing the people from Milwaukee. She couldn't quite make out what they were saying amid the other conversations being carried on in the conference room, but she could read their body language as she inched closer.

Nathan seemed calm but focused, and Sid appeared to be fretting at this latest turn of events. Kaitlin was clutching a glass and gazing up at the deputy chief with guileless eyes. Was she innocent of the attack on Georgia—or an amazing actress covering the viciousness of a murderer?

21

"Attention, please." Fergus's voice boomed over the din of conversation in the meeting room, and everyone else quieted. "Now that the police have finished here, we will begin serving dinner. I understand if anyone wants to leave. This hasn't been the Thanksgiving any of us expected."

A chorus of supportive comments quickly made it clear that the staff all planned to stay and enjoy the meal, but Kaitlin waved a hand at Fergus. "I appreciate the invitation you extended to us, but I've lost my appetite. I'm going back to the country club."

"That's understandable," Fergus said. "If you don't mind waiting a moment, I can have some food wrapped up in case you're hungry later."

Kaitlin offered him a weak smile. "That's kind of you."

Molly watched the exchange with mixed feelings. She couldn't tell if she was glad her prime suspect was leaving, or disappointed at a missed opportunity to question her.

Nathan laid a hand on Kaitlin's arm, but she roughly shrugged him off, much to Molly's surprise. "I thought I'd come with you," he said. "This is no time to be alone."

"You're mistaken." Kaitlin's angry tone was back, the one Molly had heard from her more than once. "This is exactly the time for me to be alone behind a locked door."

Molly nearly recoiled at Kaitlin's ferocity. That's a woman who could be capable of stabbing someone.

"I understand," Nathan said, dropping his voice almost too low for

Molly to hear, despite how close she'd crept to the pair. "But please let me walk you to your car at least. Someone around here is apparently very willing to hurt people."

At first, Molly thought Kaitlin was going to refuse, but then her tight shoulders slumped a bit. "Thank you. That would be kind."

Molly almost wanted to shout to Nathan that the someone he was concerned about might be Kaitlin herself. She was clearly angry with Nathan. And she might have tried to poison him before. Molly didn't want him going outside alone with her. She scanned the conference room. Fergus stood near the appetizer table, speaking with several of the servers. His face was serious, and Molly was loath to pull him away for her hunch.

She caught sight of Chloe chasing after Angus. The little dog was dashing toward the far door where Laura was standing. Molly realized with some embarrassment that she hadn't even noticed that her friend hadn't arrived yet. Molly considered enlisting Laura in her plan to watch over Nathan, but there wasn't time. Nathan and Kaitlin were already heading out the conference room's other door.

Molly pulled her phone from her small purse to text Chloe about where she was going. She slipped through the conference room door and followed Kaitlin and Nathan as she typed. *Following Kaitlin to car. Worried about Nathan.*

Dropping her phone in her purse, Molly edged into a small alcove to avoid being spotted as Nathan and Kaitlin picked up coats from the check stand. Molly knew she wouldn't be able to grab her own coat, but she doubted she'd be outside long.

The moment she stepped outside, however, Molly missed her coat badly. Kaitlin and Nathan were already nearly to the rear parking area, though, so Molly tried to forget the chill and ducked behind the shrubs where she could watch them without being easily seen. The bushes blocked some of the cold wind, and Molly huddled close to them gratefully.

In the parking lot, Nathan and Kaitlin paused for a heated conversation next to her SUV. Kaitlin didn't look at all like the pleasant woman she was capable of being. She waved her hands and occasionally poked Nathan in the chest. At first his expression was consoling, but as Kaitlin ranted at him, his face darkened.

Molly wondered if her daughter would come out to check on her. She doubted Chloe would leave her alone outside, and she was beginning to think that some backup would be a good idea. What would she do if Kaitlin actually tried to hurt Nathan? After all, Molly was fairly sure she'd tried to poison him once, and she might be concealing the knife she'd used to hurt Georgia.

Suddenly, Kaitlin gave up all pretense of calm speech and began to shout at Nathan. "You stay away from me!" she yelled. "Don't think I can't deal with you!" Kaitlin practically ripped open her car door and jumped in, slamming the door in Nathan's face.

Nathan raised his voice to be heard over the sound of her cranking the engine. "Kaitlin, come on. I only have your best interest at heart."

If Kaitlin heard him, she showed no sign. Instead, she threw the vehicle into reverse, backing out so quickly that Nathan had to jump away to avoid being smacked by her side mirror.

Nathan turned toward the building and Molly quickly ducked down, squatting to get the best cover from the bushes. Even as she moved, she couldn't help but notice the expression on Nathan's face. He wasn't merely distressed or upset—he was furious. He stormed up the sidewalk.

When he reached the part of the sidewalk closest to the bush, Molly pressed close to the bushes. She couldn't see him at all, except for one small gap that allowed her a clear view of his shoes. That's when she noticed his left pant cuff.

A single drop of dried blood stained the gray fabric.

The sight of the blood was so startling that Molly gasped aloud before throwing a hand over her mouth.

The tiny gasp was enough. Nathan rounded the bush and grabbed Molly by the arm, hauling her to her feet. "What has you so curious?" he asked her.

Before she could stop herself, her gaze flew automatically toward the blood. With his hand gripping her arm tightly, he looked down at his feet, and his face darkened even more. "I wish you hadn't seen that."

"You need to let me go," Molly said. "Or I'll scream."

Instead he hauled her closer to him and she felt the prick of something sharp in her side. He had the knife!

"Don't make a sound," he whispered as he dragged her toward his car.

Molly knew one thing without question: If she let him get her into the car, she'd never see her friends and family again. She had to get away—now. She began by dragging her feet as much as possible, stumbling frequently and making him practically hold her up to keep her moving. All the while, she searched for anyone in the area. She doubted he would stab her right in front of a witness. All she needed was one.

"You killed Camden," she said as she stumbled again, this time nearly pulling both of them over.

He hauled her viciously to her feet, and Molly knew she was going to have a spectacular bruise on her arm if she managed to get out of this.

"He forced my hand," he growled. "He found out I'd made up the dirt I gave him on your daughter. And he learned I was searching for a replacement software designer because I was sick of his drama. He threatened to break up the company rather than allow me to control his life or replace him in the company. He was going to destroy everything we'd worked for."

"Wouldn't that hurt him too?" she asked, stumbling again.

Another rough jerk. "He didn't care. He never cared about money. It was all a lark to him, a big creative lark. No, Camden would have landed on his feet. It was my life that would have been destroyed."

"You poisoned yourself to avoid suspicion."

"It worked too," he said, chuckling mirthlessly. "You bought it. You were so helpful, Molly. I'm almost sorry for what I have to do."

They'd reached the parking lot, and his grip hadn't loosened on her arm. She didn't know which car was his or how much more time she had. But she did know that the cars would offer her some protection if she could get free.

Then as they moved along the side of a gorgeous vintage truck, Molly realized that what she needed to do was surprise Nathan. She'd been dragging, making him pull her. What if she did the opposite? There was always the chance he'd simply stab her, but she suspected that was going to happen anyway. She stood up straight and threw herself into him. The knife blade raked across her ribs and she could feel it leaving a deep scratch, but Nathan jumped back in surprise, completely letting go of her.

With his grip gone, Molly flung herself on the ground and rolled beneath the high undercarriage of the truck. Nathan dropped to his knees, grabbing for her while cursing under his breath. Molly kept rolling, hoping to get out the other side and onto her feet before he could reach her.

Then to her shock, she heard the most wonderful sound in the world. Angus was barking furiously somewhere nearby.

"Mom!" Chloe screamed from the same direction.

"Hold it right there, Glower!" The deeper voice was recognizable too. Apparently the deputy chief hadn't gotten far away after all.

Whimpering with relief, Molly rolled out from under the truck.

To her surprise, Fergus was there to gather her up and lift her to her feet. He spotted the line of blood soaking through her sweater and began calling for someone to summon an ambulance.

"It's all right," Molly said. "It's only a scratch. But could we go inside? I'm freezing."

"Right away."

Fergus put his arm around her shoulders and held her so tightly as they walked that she felt almost as though he was carrying her. Finally, she felt truly safe.

After they got home from church on Sunday, Molly watched Chloe romping with Angus one last time. It was almost time for Chloe to go. Molly told herself firmly that she would not tear up.

Chloe gazed up at her and smiled, likely reading her mother's mind. "You can come visit me anytime and bring this rascal with you."

"Be careful—I may take you up on that," Molly warned her.

"I'd love it. Our Thanksgiving didn't exactly work out according to plan, but it was memorable. And I'm thankful I still have my mom."

"Georgia is going to be fine as well," Molly said. "Another thing to be thankful for."

Chloe crossed to the sofa to pick up her duffel. "And I'm thankful for my job, where we rarely want to kill one another."

Molly hugged herself. "Are you sure you have to leave today?"

"The clinic is officially a bat-free zone," Chloe said. "And they need me. Besides, I finished your book. You'll enjoy the ending. It's full of surprises."

"I don't think I'll finish it. I've had enough surprises lately." Molly opened her arms and hugged her daughter, gently since the scrape in her side was sore. "But the best one was spending Thanksgiving with you."

Chloe flashed a grin. "Even though we managed to ruin two nice outfits?"

"I can always buy more dresses," Molly said. "Ruining them was a good excuse."

Chloe chuckled then said, "Oh, this morning when I was walking Angus, I got a text from Sid."

"He texted you?"

"We had a chance to chat near the end of the strangest Thanksgiving dinner anyone had ever hosted," Chloe said. "He's nice. Anyway, he wanted to let me know his sister had her baby, and he was back in time to do some bleary-eyed babysitting."

"Oh, that's lovely," Molly said, smiling at the thought of a beautiful new baby in the world. "Did he say if it was a girl or a boy?"

"A boy. And it's not the only new boy in Sid's life."

"No?"

"He talked to Kaitlin, and apparently he's going to adopt Camden's dog, Jake. He's always wanted a dog, and he doesn't mind that Jake has food allergies."

Molly smiled. "Sid is a good guy."

"He is." Chloe hefted her bag on her shoulder. "And with that, I probably need to go."

Molly blinked rapidly, determined not to cry. "Drive carefully."

"I will." Chloe hesitated, then said, "Mom, I know you and Fergus are friends, but I think it could become something more if you encouraged it. Something wonderful."

Molly held up her hand. "I'm happy with friends. I don't want things to get complicated."

"I can understand that," Chloe agreed. "But I think you should be ready. I plan to say, 'I told you so,' when you two start dating."

Molly laughed. "You, my darling, have a vivid imagination."

"Like mother, like daughter."

On Monday afternoon after a blissfully normal workday, Molly took a box of melting moments to the hospital. She found Georgia sitting up in bed clicking the TV remote while frowning at the screen.

"I see cabin fever is setting in," Molly said from the doorway. "Care for a visitor?"

"Please, come in," Georgia said. "I flatly cannot watch any more television."

"I brought some magazines." Molly held up a selection she'd picked up at McPhee's Family Drugstore before driving over. "And cookies from the bakery."

"You are an angel," Georgia said, eagerly taking the gifts. "And not only for this. I had a visit from the deputy chief on Friday after I woke up. He said they'd caught Nathan and that you played a big part."

Molly grimaced. "It wasn't one of my finest moments. I actually thought Kaitlin was the killer."

Georgia sighed. "I thought it was the new software guy, though I couldn't come up with a good motive. But I knew Kaitlin and Nathan. At least I thought I did."

"Was Nathan the software boyfriend on your social media page?"

"He was. I'm between positions, starting at a new pharmacy next week, so I had some time off. He asked me to come here and keep Camden out of trouble. My working at Two Scots Guesthouse was his idea, but I didn't realize he'd poisoned Mrs. Loganach to make sure they needed me. That's why she was so sick and no one else caught it. No one realized it because she thought she had a regular illness and never went to the doctor. And he made your daughter sound like a monster Cam needed us to protect him from, but she's not that way at all. I should have suspected then, but Nathan said he'd made a mistake. And he could make a person believe almost anything."

"He certainly had me fooled. None of us want to think badly of the people we care about," Molly said.

"But I should have," Georgia insisted. "I knew he'd been in the guesthouse when Camden Landry died, but I believed him when he said he was concerned for Cam."

"Apparently he was concerned for what Cam intended to do to the business," Molly said.

"I finally grasped that when Nathan made it clear that he intended to let me take the blame for the murder."

"How did that happen?"

"Through some rather underhanded sneakiness, I saw the guestbook at the country club. When I saw my signature in the guestbook, I recognized Nathan's handwriting. I'd seen it often enough. He was trying to make me look guilty," Georgia said. "That opened my eyes to who he truly was."

"Well, he won't be causing any more trouble for a while," Molly said. "I have a friend in the police, and she told me that Nathan confessed to all of it. His initial plan was to kill Chloe and frame Camden, which is why he tried to burn down the bakehouse with her in it, and then to run her down with Kaitlin's SUV. He had borrowed it without asking and returned it to the guesthouse lot before it was missed. He swerved to miss her at the last second when he realized how many witnesses there were."

"So he was trying to poison Chloe at the guesthouse?" Georgia asked. "How did he get the stuff in the tea? I never took my eyes off the tray from the time I made it until I brought it out."

"Actually, the poison was all for Camden. Nathan changed his mind about setting Camden up for murder and decided he'd just kill him instead."

"What a rat!"

Molly nodded. "And the drugs weren't in the tea. Nathan poisoned Camden upstairs. He dumped some of the same drugs in the tea in the dining room after all the attention was on Camden's collapse. Then, of course, he poisoned himself to deflect police suspicion. Apparently he got the drugs from a black market seller on the Internet. He didn't say as much, but I suspect he chose poisons that were also medicines because you are a pharmacist."

"So he planned for me to take the blame for Camden's murder."

"Possibly. Though he threw plenty of blame around, especially after nearly running Chloe down with Kaitlin's vehicle."

Georgia hugged herself. "I'm grateful to be alive, even if I am stuck in here for at least another day."

Molly reached into her bag and pulled out a deck of cards. "We could play a game."

Georgia's eyes lit up. "That would be great. Though I'm afraid the only card game I know is Go Fish."

"Go Fish is one of my favorites. I used to play it all the time with Chloe."

Some of the light went out of Georgia's expression. "I'm sorry for what Nathan put Chloe through. And for the part I played in helping him."

"She doesn't hold it against you," Molly said as she took the cards from the box and began shuffling. "And we all have apologies to make. I'm sorry you were my prime suspect for a while. Nathan did a good job of making you look guilty."

"But you didn't give up on me," Georgia said. "Even when it would have been easy. That makes you one of the good guys in my book. And speaking of guys, I plan to be much more careful about the ones I get involved with in the future."

Molly laughed as she began dealing the cards. "That sounds like smart advice for all of us."

A while later, as she was walking to her car, Molly's phone beeped with an incoming call. She smiled when she saw it was a very good guy.

"Hi, Fergus," she answered brightly.

"You sound happy," he said. "What are you up to?"

"I just spent some time with Georgia at the hospital, and she's doing much better."

"That's a relief. She seems to be made of strong stuff."

"She definitely is," Molly agreed. "To what do I owe the pleasure of your call?"

"I was wondering if I could tempt you to join me for a makeup Thanksgiving dinner at Castleglen. I feel bad your holiday was ruined by all the drama."

"Yes, uncovering a murderer and having my life threatened certainly put a damper on things," she said wryly. "I'd be delighted to eat turkey and mashed potatoes with you in peace . . . as long as there's cranberry sauce too."

Fergus chuckled. "That can be arranged. How does seven o'clock sound?"

"It's a date," Molly said, then felt her cheeks warm. *A friendly date,* she told herself, though she couldn't suppress a smile. Friendly or otherwise, she could think of nothing she'd rather do that evening.